THE OTHERS FROM R.M. GILMORE

DYLAN HART

The Scene
Endless Night
Sacrifice
Forsaken
Bound
White Walls

PRUDENCE PENDERHAUS

17 Marigold Lane
19 Marigold Lane
21 Marigold Lane

And the Creek Don't Rise

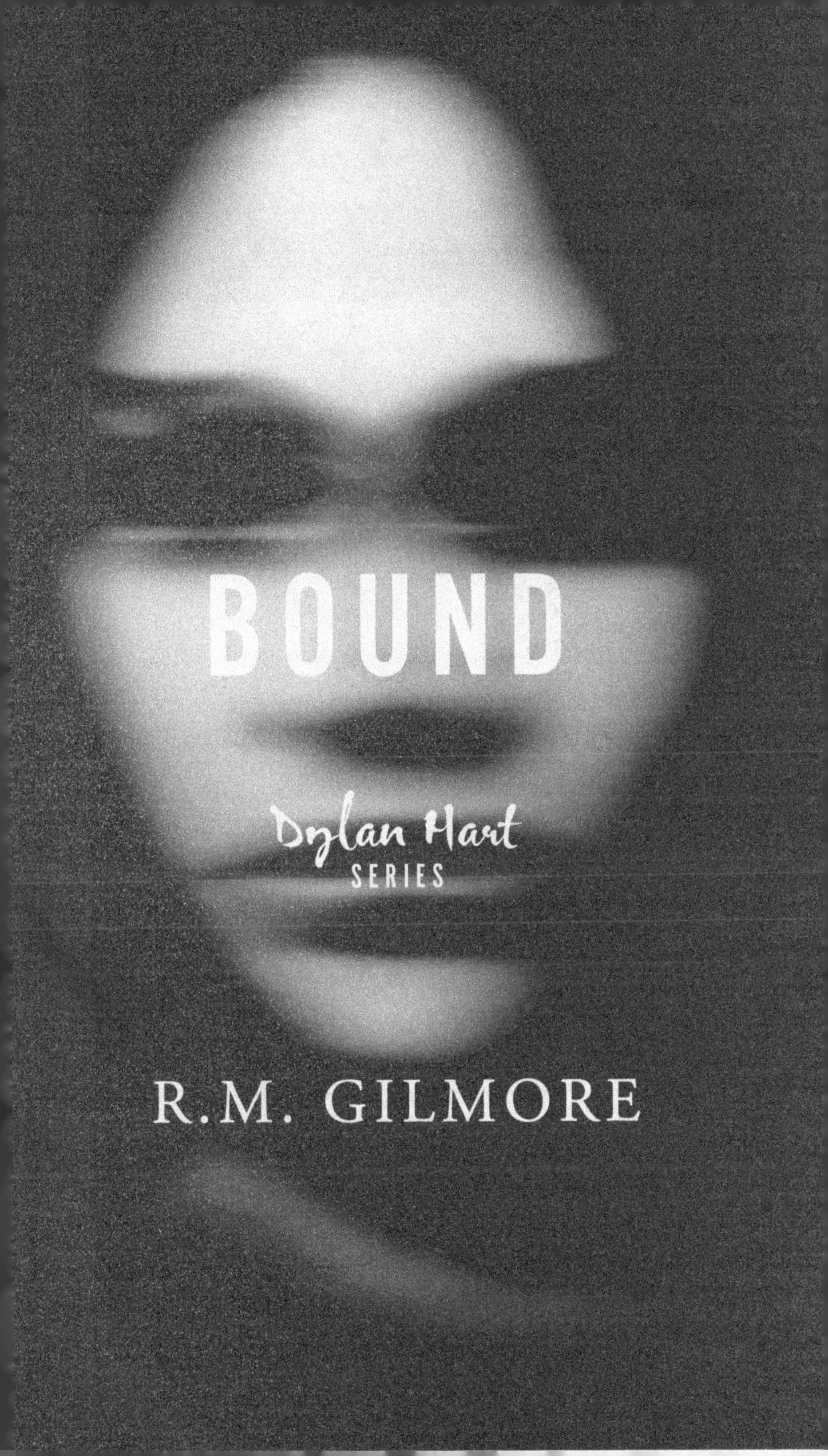
BOUND
Dylan Hart
SERIES
R.M. GILMORE

Bound by R.M. Gilmore

Anniversary Edition

Edited by Becky Johnson

Design by RMGraphX

978-1-7358635-3-5

Mac Gille Mhur Publishing

To the real Michael Petersen.
Meet you in Valhalla.

What squeals louder than a caught rat?

-Batman, *1966*

ONE

MY EYES OPENED TO DARKNESS. THE SCENT OF ROSES AND heavy spices hung thick in the air. Laying perfectly still, I didn't dare move a muscle during the long few moments it took for my brain to comprehend what was happening and figure out where I was. Vague memories of nothingness and the pungent odor of sulfur ran through my mind. Fear began to take hold.

Where the fuck am I?

Is that my *heartbeat?*

A sound I hadn't heard in what seemed to be an eternity—the beating of my own heart—thrummed in my head. I squeezed my eyes shut and focused on the beat of my heart. *Thump-thump, thump-thump*. It pounded away in my chest, proving that wherever I'd been, I was alive. Whatever had happened in the moments I was missing hadn't killed me.

Point for team Dylan.

In the pitch-dark, it was impossible to properly judge my surroundings. I did the best I could regardless, and attempted to ignore my ever-hastening heartbeat. A quick evaluation of my body proved all limbs were accounted for. Free from any bindings or straps, my arms and legs were free to pull close to my body. Head throbbing, I closed my eyes tightly against the ache. I felt like I'd just awoken from a three-day bender. As my head got its shit together, I noticed my clothes were different. My jeans and T-shirt were gone, replaced with only a tank top and underwear. Suddenly shivering, I pulled the blanket around my mostly naked body. The plush bed covering didn't budge as I tugged, and I realized something was holding the other side of the blanket taut. With memories of headless best friends and shiny black demons flashing in my head, I turned cautiously to see what was holding the material.

Tatum's sardonic smile, the clicking of the demon as it scurried through my hell, the sounds of torment flooded my memory. Not in clear, linear images, but flashes and fragments of terror popped through. Blinking away the visions, I willed my eyes to adjust to the dark.

In the darkness, it was impossible to see anything with any certainty. Every shadow could've been translated a million ways. My mind didn't have the best track record for honesty as of late, and it took everything I had not to imagine a dead best friend or a beastie, or hell, even a damned headless shambling corpse. A dark form lay next to me in the bed, over the covers. Nearly sitting, the form seemed to be leaning against the headboard, legs kicked out. Bulky and heavy on the blanket, the shadow slowly began to take shape as a man.

I sat up, eyes trained on the shadow. With no bra, my tank top had its work cut out for it holding back my boobs. Sliding one bare leg from under the blanket, I silently lowered my foot to the carpeted floor. The form didn't move. I lifted my body off the bed, momentarily balancing on one foot until the other slid off the edge. The moment both feet were safely on the ground, I released a long relieved breath.

Shadows held the room hostage, allowing me to only see in vague highlights. In that lighting, everything in the room seemed like it could've been a door. Judging by the placement of the bed and the old-lady smell, I was fairly certain I didn't recognize the space.

With hands spread wide in front of me, I searched blindly; groping the heavy blackness. I shuffled forward, using the edge of the bed as a guide against my bare right leg and moving no more than a foot at a time, making my way along the edge of the bed.

At the corner, my tender, cold pinky toe slammed into something solid and immobile. The entire bed shook with the inertia. I reached and grasped the bedpost I'd run into. Steadying the bed and myself. Holding the post for stability, I rubbed my toe and tried not to cry. After all I'd been through, and a damn stubbed toe about destroyed me.

I cautiously worked my way around the person-high corner post, walking mostly on my heel. From the farthest wall, the slightest sliver of light glinted. Brass, maybe silver. A doorknob? That was where I was headed.

Leaving the safety of the bedpost behind, I ventured into

the darkness alone. Though I moved cautiously, feeling my way through empty air, it wasn't enough. The *thunk* came before the pain. A zinging shock pulled bile up my throat and a whispered curse from my lips as it rocked through my right leg. I sucked air in through my clenched teeth, and I grabbed my aching toe. The damn thing couldn't take another blow.

With nothing to cling to, I quickly lost my balance. I fell forward. My open hands and rigid arms caught me against the low cushioned object I'd inadvertently kicked.

The shadowy form lying in bed snorted loudly. I yelped and turned quickly toward the snort as it leapt from the bed. My heart dropped to the floor. I spun around again, this time toward the shard of light. I hoped was a door. My knee caught the edge of whatever I'd stubbed my toe against, and I tumbled over the top of it.

Toe throbbing, knees screaming out in agony, I forced my tired body to scramble to its feet. I reached out, desperate for the smooth metal finish of a doorknob. A light clicked on behind me, and my shadow fell over a white door only a few feet away from me. I lunged toward it, reaching as far as my fingers would allow, desperate for freedom.

"Dylan," a voice, so full of desperation it nearly broke my heart, called out to me.

I stopped dead, my hand still reaching for the knob. My heart leapt with relief, dancing in my chest, but my head refused to accept it. The images locked in my mind were jumbled, and my memory was anything but accurate, but the lingering feeling of panic and terror clung to me like a shit-sucking June bug to sweaty skin. Fear refused to allow my brain to believe what it'd just heard.

Panic was setting in. I held my breath. My heart galloped an unhealthy cadence in my chest. Pushing my eyes far to the peripheral, I tried to make out the face before my body turned completely, before I allowed myself to believe it was true. Shadows fell over his face, morphing handsome features into monstrous forms. But it was him. In the flesh.

I turned and faced him dead on. Standing a handful of feet away, Mike stood beside the bed, hands pressed to the sides of his head. His eyes frantically searched my face for something; maybe he was searching for me. His reaction threatened to overwhelm my mounting terror.

My chin quivered with the threat of tears. Something had gone wrong. What I remembered was wrong. Mike's expression said everything. He almost looked… *afraid* of me.

Is this my true hell? Does he finally see me for the beast I've become?

"Is this real life?" I asked, cringing at the pathetic tone of my trembling voice.

"I hope so." His answer didn't fill me with confidence.

"I have to tell you, I'm really fucking scared right now." My body continued where my chin had left off and shuddered through to the bone.

He shook his head over and over in disbelief. "You have no idea." His hands slid down his face, pulling hard against the long stubble on his jaw.

Shivering uncontrollably, I did my best to stutter out something coherent. "M-m-mike, what's g-g-g--going on?" was all I could get out, though my thoughts rang succinctly in my head, my mouth refused to form the words. *I don't know where I am, I don't know what the fuck happened to me, and I don't know why you look so damn terrified.*

Shock set in. He didn't move. Not sure he even breathed. I stared at him, hands lax at my sides, lost and falling further away as the seconds ticked on. He stared at me, blinked a few times, and snapped into action. Swooping up a small blanket from the foot of the bed, Mike moved swiftly toward me. He wrapped the blanket around my shoulders, enveloping me in it and his arms.

"Lay down. Just lay down," he repeated gently.

Blankly, I followed his lead. Mike walked me to the bed, and I let him. He guided me to sit on the edge and lay back where he'd been snoozing when I woke him up. He pulled the covers back and tucked me back in. In any other circumstance, I would never have behaved so pitifully, but I'd been to Hell and back and deserved a nervous breakdown.

"What"—*gulp of air*—"happened?" I sucked oxygen into my lungs hard exhaled slowly, trying to calm myself.

Mike crawled over the top of my legs and nestled beside me. "I have no idea." His warm hand squeezed my arm, giving me something pure to cling to. "You were here one minute and the next," he sighed, "not." He breathed against my hair. "I couldn't believe she'd actually done it until I realized she hadn't." *Hadn't done what?* "Not exactly." *Spit it out, man!* "Lupe dropped the chair, but it didn't fall."

What chair? My mind flooded with memories. Lupe. A bag of dirt. A braid in my hair. My bare feet on the ground. And the chair. The chair that I knew had fallen. "But…." I pulled the memory out from the depths. It had fallen, I hit the ground and continued to fall, past the chair and the floor, further into the darkness. So long and so far until I thought I had died and that was my afterlife. Falling through darkness for eternity, my own personal hell.

"It, *you*, just floated there." He pulled a wild strand of hair from my face. "Like magic, honest to God magic, the back two legs of the chair held tight to the floor, teetering on the edges." His strong arms squeezed me tightly. "The back of the chair hovered inches above the floor." The chair had fallen, it just never hit. "Your crazy hair spilled over the floor. I held my breath waiting for you to hit the floor. Minutes went by and nothing happened. Lupe watched you for hours, covering you in rose water and lighting candles, but nothing happened. It was like someone paused the motion just seconds before the chair hit the floor. You didn't move. Didn't breathe. To us, you were dead."

"There are so many images in my head, flashes of terror and nothingness, but none of them make sense. I know I fought. I fought hard," I recalled. "But I can't tell you what happened next." I let out a breath. "It's just… gone."

"An hour before a full day had passed, the chair fell. It hit the ground with a *thunk,* and every one of us jumped. We thought you'd open your eyes and talk to us, but you didn't. You didn't do anything."

A full day?

"How long have I been gone?"

"It's Tuesday." He paused to count it out. "A little over three days."

"*Three* days?" I exclaimed and sat up. "What the fuck have I been doing for three days?"

He sat up too. "Dylan, I'm not really an expert, but if you wanted my opinion as a decorated police officer, you were dead."

I turned my head slowly to meet his eyes. "And you were lying in bed with me?" The idea wasn't the strangest thing I'd encountered in a year, but the image of Mike cuddling up to my dead body gave me the heebie-jeebies.

"What else was I supposed to do?" He flopped back against the headboard. "You woke up, didn't you?" I heard his hands scrub down his day-old beard behind me. "Obviously, dead really doesn't mean what it used to mean." That was the understatement of the century.

"You've been here… with me… for three days?" He nodded. "Where's here?"

"Sween." Made sense. "We couldn't exactly move you. You were, for all intents and purposes, dead. No breathing, no heartbeat, nothing." It threatened to stop again if Mike kept it up. "Lupe swore you weren't dead. I begged someone to call an ambulance. Almost called myself a few times." Nothing short of Lupe would have been able to stop him. A scene which I am devastated to have missed. "She promised you were just on vacation."

"Vacation?" I choked.

"That's what she called it." *Enjoy your fabulous vacation in flame drenched Hades!* "Your body was here, but your soul was out on *vacation*. Except when she said it there was more Spanish involved."

Sounds about right.

My skin jumped, quaking around my tired, trembling muscles . "I haven't moved in three days?" Having not moved for days, I was exhausted. "Not a breath? In three days." I let my body flop lazily onto the bed. Mike looked down at me and shook his head. "If this were primetime television, a new slayer would be headed this way."

Mike scrunched his face up, not fully comprehending my pop culture reference. How could I ever explain where I'd been? That, for all intents and purposes, I *was* dead. Closing my eyes, I shook my head, waving off the comment. My head swam with the notion of missing days of my life. No focus in the world—this or the next—could have forced the images locked in my head to piece themselves together properly.

"I feel hungover," I croaked. "Like I've been roofied or something."

His blue eyes stared at me, digging deep. "I thought you were dead." I looked away, unable to accept myself in his eyes. "Where did you go?"

"Ha!" I scoffed, shaking my head. "You wouldn't believe me if I told you. Hell, I don't even believe my own memories anymore."

"I don't know what to believe anymore." *Is there an echo?* "I know you were dead as a fucking doornail. I know I've watched you kill people." Darkness churned in my soul. "Both on your own accord and someone else's." Azelie played a major role in the killing of my best friend. I was just the conduit. "I know there's so much I don't know," he admitted. "I know you've changed. What I don't know is how. How did all of this happen? Who started this all?" He sighed and looked away from me. "Who the fuck took out Reggie and the other girls? Why are they important? How am I supposed to solve all of this and keep you alive at the same time?" Frustrated hands raked down his face. "A million questions and not one fucking answer."

I scoffed. I may not have known who the first vampire was or who made him—*or her*—but I sure as fuck knew who we could blame for the shit heap we were trapped in. "Azelie d'Entremonte and her blood minions. A million questions and *one* fucking answer."

"Tell me how Azelie is dead, and new bodies are popping up across the country?" Something was afoot while I was away. "Tell me how we ended up *here* without Azelie or her head?"

Because Azelie isn't the only witch bitch I've pissed off recently.

"Jim Jones. Purple Kool-Aid. It's a fucking cult, man. Who knows? Who cares? I'm so far past headless dead broads at this point." He scowled at me. "Trust me, I have more shit on my plate than these people killing each other off. I'm sorry if I'm not Miss Fresh-From-Hell Congeniality."

I swallowed back the guilt that crept up my throat. It wasn't that I didn't care about those girls, but I didn't even know what day it was, fuck, I didn't know who the hell I was anymore. I didn't have room to care. The deaths of those girls were on the bottom of my shit-to-fix list.

"Where's Cyrus and Lupe?" I asked from left field.

"Lupe's… wherever Lupes go when they're not here, doing Lupe stuff. I really can't answer that. She's been gone since the chair fell. Cyrus is at Embrace, I assume. I'm sure he's avoiding me and not you, but he's been there more than here. Said he had some Primus shit to take care of." He lowered his voice. "We had no idea if… *when* you'd wake up. Everyone had to get back to their lives for a while." His tone suggested I was supposed to feel abandoned because people didn't sit and watch my mostly dead body.

"Everyone but you," I said. Before he could reply, I added, "It's fine," having no energy to deal with his reasoning. "There's no reason any one of you should have waited on a dead girl to wake up anyway." Doing some avoiding of my own, I slid off the edge of the bed and padded across the floor. Mania was setting in. Whatever was happening to my head didn't have clear steps or stages to breathe and count to ten. "I really, really just want something normal right now." I didn't have any reason to leave the bed, so I made something up on the fly before he got suspicious. "Can you please help me find my pants?"

"Dylan, I think you should just rest for a while. I'm certain there are some serious medical issues a professional should be tending to, but I'm willing to put that aside in exchange for a little cooperation. Lay down and let your body recover." He sat up and tossed his long legs over the edge of the bed. "Are your pants really a priority?"

"Michael, I'm hanging on by a thread here." I huffed. "Pants, now." Irrational panic bubbled up and shook my chin again. I didn't know really why I was standing or why my pants suddenly took precedence over anything else, but in that moment, it was the most rational thing I could've done.

He sat on the edge of the bed and pulled my jeans from

under a pile of his stuff stacked on the nightstand. "Here." I jerked my pants from his grasp. "Now, will you please sit down and relax." He dropped his head to his hands, running thick fingers through his hair. "I guess I need to call Cyrus." He let out a begrudging sigh at the idea of calling in the reinforcements. "And probably Lupe." Not only was Mike not the type to elicit help, he sure as fuck wasn't interested in getting it from the magical duo.

I slid into my filthy jeans, hopping a bit to shove my ass in all the way. They buttoned easily, and I realized I'd shrunk at least an inch. I reveled in the idea for only a second before my stomach rumbled painfully and I was taken over by the need for sustenance.

"I want food. Now." I growled angrily and shocked myself. He looked at me from the corners of his suspicious eyes while holding the phone to his head. Plopping on the edge of the bed, I kept my distance from Mike's distrustful glare.

Someone answered on the other end. "She's up," he said and hung up the phone. It was clear he and Cyrus hadn't bonded during my time away. My stomach groaned and Mike pulled his brows together. "Yeah. Yeah, you're probably pretty hungry." The suspicion in his eyes hurt. I hadn't meant to sound like a hell bitch; it just came out that way. Jet lag.

Dead lag?

"Sorry," I said quickly, looking away. I wasn't really sorry of course, and really, I had no idea why I chose to apologize. I was fucking hungry. I was fucking tired. And I was fucking scared. Three things you didn't want Dylan Hart to be.

He stood, tucking his phone into his back pocket. I lifted

myself off the bed instinctively to follow him out of the room, but he stepped in front of me, and I was suddenly nose deep into his vast chest. Hunger growled deep inside and, as I let my eyes trail up his body, I seriously considered eating him alive.

"I know this was something you had to do, but I want this to all just be over. I want you back to being normal you. Because I'll be honest, this vampire, ghost, demon, *X-Files* shit is way, way too Joss Whedon for me."

Unexpected fury churned lava down in my depths. I looked up at him under my brows. "Fine," I said through my teeth.

Just, fucking, feed me.

He lowered his face close to mine, cradling a hand at the nape of my neck. "No more fighting." He kissed my forehead. "For any of us."

Quietly, I hoped that were true and desperately fended away the urge to gnaw his ear off.

Hangry Dylan is a dangerous bitch.

TWO

I WAS HALFWAY THROUGH A DELI PACK OF SALAMI WHEN boisterous preternatural beings, whom I'd begun to rely on with my life, barreled through the front doors of Sween.

"Aye, boy, did you get here any faster?" Lupe scolded Cyrus as they burst into the house. "Like a rollercoaster. The girl isn't going anywhere. *Hijo de la chingcada.* You could have killed me." Her wooden leg clunked against the hardwood with each sure step. At the very least that calamity hadn't changed. I looked on at the scene, grateful for a glimpse of my new normal. Whatever the fuck that had become. In that moment, I considered poking out the magically repaired eye, just for the chance to see the peg leg and patch combo in the hobbling flesh.

"Dylan," Cyrus said, covering Lupe's moving, flapping

mouth with his hand.

I bobbed my head once. “Oh, hey,” I said, my mouth full of greasy meat someone had purchased in the days I’d been away.

Cyrus stared at me with eyes so green they were hard to look at. “This is… remarkable,” he admired, hand still clamped over Lupe’s wrinkled lips.

“Get your hands off me.” Lupe batted him away. “You don’t believe me. See? You see? On vacation,” she said under her breath as she tottered over to me. “Let me look at you.” Lupe grasped my face roughly with her withering hands. Cyrus’s magic juice had done the trick. She still looked twenty years younger than she had—which was still easily over sixty—but her hands were rough and leathery still. Not old, just aged.

“I feel hungover.” I shoved another piece of meat in my mouth. “And hungry.”

She nodded, her thick salt-and-pepper bun bounced on her head. “Should clear up in a day or two.”

“Take an aspirin and suck it up. You’re back from Hell, sweetie. Life’s going to suck for a while.” Dominika slinked into the room behind the *thunking* old lady and flopped onto the couch beside me. Her skintight blue dress clung to her curves.

“Thanks for the tip. Look, I can’t remember anything. I can hardly remember why I’m here in the first place. I get I was basically dead for the better part of three days, but is this shit permanent?” I waved a greasy hand over my sloppy body and wondered for a moment whether or not that mattered to me. So I couldn’t recall the horrendous events of my trip to hell? Poor me.

Lupe turned the corners of her mouth down, tilting her head back and forth. “Probably not.”

“Oh, wonderful.” I pushed another slice into my mouth.

"Can someone please get me up-to-date?"

"Your face is greasy, your hair is atrocious, and you're in desperate need of a shower."

"Dominika, you have no idea how you've helped the situation." She raised an uninterested eyebrow and examined her nails. "Why is she even here?" I asked, thumbing her direction.

"Had to see the hell bitch for myself. You're quite the conundrum, peaches." Puckering her lips, she closed her sultry eyes and blew me a contentious kiss.

I lowered my brows and glowered at her. "You don't know how right you are." All eyes moved toward me. No one asked, but their thoughts dug under my skin like fleas. "I fell. The chair stopped, but I kept going. I fell into the darkness until I thought I was stuck in limbo and there would be no end to my descent." Mike scooted to the edge of the chair he'd pulled over. My mind involuntarily flashed on Tatum and the beasty. "She wasn't there," I recalled. Lupe's face pulled inward as she wrinkled her brow. I shook my head. "She wasn't there. It was just… *him*."

"Him?" Mike asked.

"That thing. That… *demon*." I shook my head, forcing the image from my mind. "It never had her. She was never *here*." My heart sank at the thought that the comfort I'd felt in hearing the voice of my best friend was nothing more than a ruse put forth by a spawn from hell. Or there was always the possibility I was just a fucking nutbag.

"Then why…?"

"Me. He wanted me." I didn't know why or recall any specific details, but I knew that son of a bitch had tricked me. I knew that for whatever reason, it was me he'd been hunting.

"Well?" Dominika asked. I stared at her, unsure what her *well* meant. "Did you kill it?" Her accent stretched the i in *kill* out longer than necessary.

A flash of the beastly thing shrieking and flailing about rocked my senses. I closed my eyes against it and rubbed my forehead. Dirt filled its mouth. I'd shoved my bag of dirt into his face, and he thrashed around in pain and protest. "I don't know. I think so." I held my head in my hands. "I've been awake for a few hours, and I haven't heard from her… *it* at all." Speaking of Tatum brought a lump to my throat. "That has to be a good sign. Right?"

"Oh, that reminds me… Dylan, hon," Mike spoke softly, "New Orleans released Tatum to me yesterday."

A solid *thunk* hit my gut at the sound of her name. Detective Colorado had finished his investigation of her remains and had no further use for her body. I didn't have words. What did you say to something like that? "Okay." I swallowed down the lump. It stuck in my chest and sat there to fester, wavering between sadness and rage. "What the fuck am I supposed to do now?" A hot tear slid down my cheek.

"A nap, perhaps?" Dominika sarcastically suggested.

I snarled in her direction.

"Dylan, a rest wouldn't hurt." Cyrus crouched in front of me, his piercing eyes level with mine. "I know you've been… away for a long time, but it is doubtful your mind was at ease in that time." His warm hands slid over the tops of mine. "Despite what you'll admit, you've been through more than most humans can handle and at neck-breaking speeds. Dear, you've dipped your toes into the abyss of the otherworld. You might be a bit dehydrated."

A smirk tugged at the corners of my mouth. Under all the

shock, the filth, the stench of hell was Dylan Hart. Somewhere. Down deep, perhaps. How to get her out?

Put some water on it.

"Let me run you a bath and get you out of those dirty clothes." Cyrus stood and took my hands with him.

Mike glared at me over Cyrus's shoulder. A flash of me frantically kissing Mike in the foyer hit my memory, and I was instantly reminded of the promise I'd made to Mike. The promise I'd love him until the day I died. An arrogant smile spread across my face as I thought of all the delicious ways I could make good on that promise.

"A bath would be stellar, but I can get myself out of these dirty-ass clothes."

Cyrus nodded once, and Mike's glare faded quickly as he leaned back in the chair, kicking out one leg as a show of dominance. It was a masculine, cocky movement meant only for the other man in the room.

Cyrus nodded quickly. "Yes. Yes." He released my hands and didn't so much as glance over his shoulder before he scuttled off upstairs.

Once he was clear of earshot, I asked, "What's up his ass?" I nodded in his direction.

Dominika's thin eyebrows raised dramatically as she lowered her lids. "Your boyfriend and his men in uniforms threw the book at him." I wondered how many episodes of Matlock she'd seen before that phrase stuck. "He's also under scrutiny from the Southern Cabal due to the sudden disappearance of their Primus, Marienne Poisson, and your favorite pal, Malcolm McTavish. Quite the scandal."

Mike stood in defense of himself and his boys in blue. "His *little bar* was violating half-a-dozen city codes. Someone *else* caught on when they shut them down last week."

"Last week?" I scoffed. Seemed like hours, maybe a day, but a week? "A nap indeed."

Moments later, Cyrus called to me from the top of the stairs. Not a moment too soon. Mike and Dominika had been locked in a staring contest I was certain would end in bloodshed, and I did not have time or energy for that nonsense. No one spoke as I stood and left them for my bath. They all eyed each other when I moved past them and toward the stairs, as though they were waiting for me to leave the room to talk about grown-up things. The room remained silent behind me as I headed upstairs and out of earshot.

Passing me on the stairs, Cyrus stopped suddenly and wrapped strong arms around me. Something I was certain Mike would have frowned at. He didn't say a word, only gave a tight squeeze and a sigh before continuing his descent.

Beyond the space I recalled as once being filled with industrial lighting and beautiful people, the open bathroom door beckoned. The door to what was once Malcolm's office loomed over me as I walked past. I ignored my curiosity begging me to open it. I shook my head and refused to give in. That room held a memory I'd just as soon forget. Whatever was up in that room could stay put. I had enough on my plate to curb my officious nature for the rest of my life.

Once alone in the quiet of the bathroom, I slid out of my filthy jeans and white tank. Cyrus had filled the massive claw-foot tub nearly to the brim with steaming hot water. Vanilla-scented bubbles billowed over the edges, threatening to spill over.

I dipped a toe and pulled it out quickly against the heat. It was hot enough to melt the stench of hell right off. The water scalded my skin, but I pushed through it and stepped in with both feet. My feet turned a lobster shade of red that crept up toward my knee.

Standing naked in the knee-deep water, waiting for my body to adjust to the temperature, I caught sight of my own reflection in the mirror. I didn't look any different. I didn't look like someone who'd just come back from a trip to hell, or wherever I'd been since heaven and hell weren't really a thing.

Checking my physique, I pulled my chubby stomach in tight. After a moment or two of no oxygen, I let it loose and snarled at my own gut. "How's that salami, ol' girl?" I patted it and shook my head at its size. "Who fucking cares?" I asked myself about the appearance of my body. I didn't. Not really. Not deep down inside. Not anymore. Fat shamers took a backseat to zombies and voodoo curses and trips to the underworld. Mike wanted me. He wasn't a troll by any means, and he wanted me fat or not. And Cyrus, well.... Besides, in the long run, what was a chunky ass when all was said and done? I was three-days dead either way.

Three-days dead plays hell on the body.

Having had enough of my own odd body, I sank tits deep into the steamy water. It stung all the tender parts until I was neck deep and breathing through the pain. As far as baths went, it wouldn't have been anything to write home about had it not been for my aching muscles and frazzled nerves. Not even a minute in the water and my knotted ends unraveled, ten more and I would have been a human noodle. I closed my eyes and allowed the warmth of the water to settle my churning soul. My muscles, having not used them in days, were tight and whined with each movement.

Vanilla scented bubbles covered my naughty bits and filled the room with a delicious aroma that made my stomach growl. Eventually I would need a real meal, preferably with bacon.

It seemed hypersleep was confined to movies. Unconscious or not, three days of no food or other means of sustenance would have consequences. Uncontrollable hunger at the smell of vanilla was definitely not a good sign.

In the silence of the bathroom, steam filling the air, I was granted a few moments reprieve from my hellish existence. Nothing chased me. Nothing burst through the door. The smell of gunpowder and blood didn't fill my nose. I was just Dylan Hart, woman of earth. That was until the scent of vanilla disappeared and another, unearthly familiar aroma wafted through. I opened my eyes quickly, searching the room for who logic told me should have been there. As far as I could tell in the dim light, I was alone. The smell of my dad's cologne still lingered in the air; an unseen ghost of a memory.

On the counter, a tall blue pillar candle sat unlit. Aside from the decorative towels and soaps, the candle was the only thing in the room that could have been putting off the scent. Curiosity overcame me in only a breath, and I hoisted my wet body from the tub and braved the cold room to snatch the candle from the counter to give it a smell. Clutching it in slippery hands, I breathed it in. *Lavender*.

I looked around the room for any hint that I had a long-awaited visitor. Only bathroom things and me took up the space. Shaking away the feeling I wasn't alone, I slid back into the tub and let out a long breath.

"Get it together," I whispered. I wanted it all to be over. Wished it with everything that made me up as a human being.

Vanilla filled my nose again and once more I sank deep into

the water. I didn't dare dunk my head into the bath completely, my poor scalp would have to wait until I was home to get a good scrubbing. There wasn't enough product in the world that could fix the mess water and random bubble bath would create.

"Frizzle." A breath of a whisper hung in the air.

I sat up frantically, water splashed out of the tub and soaked the floor. "Dad?" I panted. No response. "Daddy?" I pleaded, my voice a tiny whimper.

I was nearly hanging out of the tub, clinging to the edge, pleading with my eyes to see a man logic told me wouldn't be there.

The soft, golden pink light flickered overhead. It buzzed louder and louder over a second or two. The smell of spent gunpowder hit my senses a moment before the bulb burst in its housing and the room went from dim to dark in a blink. With no windows for light to penetrate, I sat alone in the tub in the pitch-black.

"Fuck," I breathed. Heart thudding in my chest, my mind instantly imagined all the ghostly bad things waiting for me in the dark. "Dad," I whimpered, "if you're really here, please, just don't scare me. I don't think this old ticker can take it," I begged, sliding cautiously from the tub.

Wet feet squeaked against the tile floor as I moved slowly toward the counter. Feeling out in front of me with open hands, I searched for the lavender candle. My fingertips grazed the waxy surface, and it toppled over, tumbling off the counter and onto the floor. Hands trembling from the cold and the fear, I searched the countertop for the book of Embrace matches I'd seen sitting beside the candle.

Gingerly, so not to knock anything breakable off the counter, I felt over the smooth surface until my fingertips found purchase on the small rectangle box. Naked, cold, and scared of the dark, I knelt on the tile and crawled across the wet floor in search of the fallen candle. As I scooted along the tiles, I told myself to crawl for the door and let in the light—call for Mike or Cyrus and they'd come running. But I didn't do any of that. I wanted to see him with my own eyes. I needed to know he was there with me. And if he wasn't, I needed to know what was before calling in the reinforcements.

Against the baseboard of the far wall, I found the candle. I blew on my wet fingers to dry them before striking the match and lighting the wick. Shaking hands slid a wooden match over what I hoped was the striker on the side of the box. Nothing. I sat back on my heels and tried again. Flame plumed from the end of the matchstick. Blackness loomed over me, swiping the flame and stealing the light.

I swallowed hard against ragged breaths. Pulling one more match from the box, I tried one last time. Strike, flame, light. Holding my breath, I touched the flame to the wick of the candle. It lit and filled the room with fragrance and flickering light.

Hand trembling, I held the lit candle out in front of me. "Dad," I called desperately to him. "Please come back." I waited for never-ending seconds, but nothing came. "Don't leave me."

A few minutes passed, and nothing came for me. Dad wasn't there anymore, and I worried he really never had been. If he hadn't, one of two things were happening, either I had hallucinated the whole thing which meant I really was a fucking nutbag, or my torment hadn't ended when I left the confines of my very own personal hell. Neither of which I was looking forward to telling the people downstairs.

"She's just tired," Mike defended as I passed the head of the stairs on my way to the bedroom after an unfortunately short soak in the tub.

I stood motionless at the top of the stairs, *innocently overhearing* their conversation. Water dripped from the back of my ponytail and fell onto my bare shoulders, sending a shudder down my spine. I hadn't wanted to put my dirty clothes back on and hoped there was something by way of fat-girl coverings somewhere in the house. With nothing more than a towel wrapped around my body, visions of ghostly daddies in my head, and the stench of hell clinging to my clean skin, I'd inadvertently stumbled upon a conversation about me—clearly I had to stop and listen. Right?

"That may be so, but you can't discount the stench rolling off her." Dominika's thick accent set her voice apart from the others easily, but was more difficult to decipher as it wafted up the staircase.

"She hasn't bathed in days. What do you expect?" Mike defended me against Dominika's insults.

"The stench of death, Detective," Dominika interjected. "She wreaks of the otherworld. A foul strangling stench I cannot believe you don't smell."

I sniffed my vanilla-scented pits. No different than before I'd taken my magical mystery ride, I didn't smell anything. But I did vaguely remember Mike commenting on my mysterious odor at Embrace during the big raid.

"I'm sorry. My poor, pathetic human nose isn't as fancy

as your vampire-bitch-with-a-tight-fucking-bun-and-stupid-looking-face-nose."

What? What the hell was that?

Stifling a laugh, I leaned in further to better catch every word. *Innocently.*

"Dominika, let it go," Cyrus said, expressing his newfound diplomacy. "Michael, I know this isn't easy for you, but we all have to accept whatever comes to pass from here on out. Dylan, though horrendously stupid in her choices, has come back from something not a one of us standing here can imagine. She herself has blocked out most of the ordeal. With the funeral plans needing to be made and a dear friend to put in the dirt, can we all agree it's best for Dylan if those images she has locked away in her head stay there?"

Funeral plans.

I had to plan a funeral. Cyrus was right. It would have been better to just let whatever happened stay locked away in my head. It was over. It was time to move along and let it all go. Time to let *her* go.

"For the time being," Cyrus added.

"Yes," Mike said quietly. He sniffed back what sounded like could've been the start of tears. "Whatever we have to do to get her back I'll do it. It's all just been too much. Too much for anyone. Let alone someone who killed their…." He let himself trail off.

"I know." Cyrus's voice sounded uncharacteristically gloomy.

"There are so many deaths at her hand," Lupe added. "So many moments of supernatural intrusion in her soul." She sounded as though she was in deep thought, talking to mostly herself. "She may be suffering a souring. A trip to the otherworld can do that from time to time with the purest of souls. Taking into account the wretched marks on her soul, her stench may only be the beginning."

Beginning of what? This was supposed to be the end of it all. What happened to a day or two?

"She seems fine," Mike denied. "Just tired. And hungry. She was starving. She hadn't eaten in days. Can we not jump to horrific mystical conclusions just yet? Can we please just give her some time to be normal?" Count on Mike to want me to be normal. That was all he'd ever wanted. Before all the vampire, voodoo, beheading crap even. Just be normal.

"Aye, but don't let it leave your mind completely. A soured soul is a dying heart. If she has brought hell back in her wake, it won't take long to show its face."

I felt fine, with the exception of the splitting headache and possible hallucinations. Tired, just like Mike said. I was exhausted. And yes, hungry. So very hungry. Okay, and maybe a little scared, too. The bath had helped. I didn't smell like three-day-dead vagina anymore. I was, however, still naked.

Silence fell over them. "Hey, guys," I called down the stairs after a few minutes of waiting in silence.

Scuffling, hurried footsteps led Mike to the foot of the stairs. "Yeah?" He looked up, eyes wide at the sight of me in a towel. "Coming right up." He smiled and hurried up the steps, and it brought a blush to my cheeks.

"No, no, no. I just need some clothes." I held my hands up, warding off his poorly timed advances.

"No, you don't." His smile widened as he got closer to me on the stairs.

"Do you really think now's the time for this?" I asked as he slid his hands around my waist.

"You're alive. You're clean. You're naked. Is there a better time?"

He had a point. There was still that pesky otherworld jet lag and my newfound fear of the unknown. "How about when we're alone?" I said, eyeing the base of the stairs.

"Got it." He stepped forward, forcing me to step backward.

"What are you doing?"

"Making us alone." He pushed the bedroom door open and walked us through it.

The hunger that had consumed me when I woke hadn't been quenched completely by greasy salami and flared up again under his touch. This time, however, the hunger wasn't for food. It wasn't for anything I could eat outright. It was for him.

"And you think this is a good idea right now?" I couldn't keep the smile off my face. An ache rolled through my body, a hunger pang like no other. "Mike, I—"

His mouth found mine with ease. Old hat, kissing Michael Petersen. Passionate hunger crept up my legs and into my core reminding me of the night I'd tried to sleep with Cyrus in the middle of Embrace. The same hunger. The same innate need to devour him. No, not him exactly. Devour anything.

"Okay, lover boy." I pushed him away gently. My mind flashing on the black beast I'd fended off and the hunger it had brought out in me. "Save it for later." A sullen frown developed on his face and tugged my apathetic heartstrings. "Later," I promised and kissed him once more to seal the deal. "Promise."

"Then you better put some clothes on that ass." Smiling sourly, he rifled through the stack of his shit on the side table and pulled out a pair of sweats and a T-shirt. "Here. Until we can get you home."

"Thanks," I said dryly, and I examined the wad of cloth he'd tossed at me.

"Don't forget your bling, Flavor Flave." Condescendingly, he tossed the golden medallion to me. With reflexes I didn't recognize as my own, I caught Lupe's Devil's Trap with one hand. "Nice catch, Dwight Clark." His football reference didn't go unnoticed, but I ignored the testosterone-induced tease. He was pissed he didn't get laid. *Join the club.* I wanted to ease his tension by ensuring him I had every intention to strip him down and have my way with him, but I didn't, for more reasons than I could plausibly name. The main, usually subconscious, reason being my innate desire to fuck my life up.

In no mood for his bullshit, I scowled as I held up the nondescript grey sweats and faded Pixies shirt. Although I'd have to roll up the legs, my fat ass would fit into his clothes well enough for the day. *Gee, thanks for bringing me my very own clothes from my very own house ten minutes away from your house*. "Guess I'm going commando," I said bitterly.

"Guess so." He gave me a cocky slap on the ass and left the room.

As long as life kept moving forward, I'd have that man naked before the week was up. I made myself that one promise. Knowing my luck, it would be the last romp I'd ever have. Or I'd be dragged back to hell and cursed with eternal blue balls.

"Fashion Week came early."

"Can someone tell her to fuck off? I don't have the energy," I grumbled, coming down the stairs in my all-too comfortable ensemble.

"Feeling better?" Cyrus asked, nervous tension screaming through his words.

"I don't stink anymore." I shrugged.

"Really?" Dominika asked under her breath.

I shot her a glare and Cyrus stepped between us. "Wonderful." His face suddenly softening, his eyes focused on my mouth. "What would you like now?"

I sighed, thinking for a moment about what my soul needed. "My house." All eyes fell on me. "Oh fuck, come on," I exclaimed at their reaction. "What did it, like, implode into another dimension or something?" I joked. No one spoke. "Did it?"

"No," Mike answered. "It's your mom." I raised a concerned eyebrow. "She thinks you're in Tahoe."

"So? I'm home now." I stopped auto-pilot and shot my gaze to Mike.

Tahoe?

"With me." Mike let out a loud breath. "She was so worried when you didn't answer your phone, *her* phone. What was I supposed to say?"

"Uh, how about anything other than Tahoe with you. You know that if she thinks I'm in Tahoe with you, she thinks we fucking eloped or something." Mike's eyes looked to the floor. "Or *something*." I pushed.

"I didn't specify anything," he defended. "She wouldn't just believe you were fine. I told her I took you to Tahoe because you needed to get away from all this. A few reporters called your mom's, one showed up at the door on the first morning you were gone. Tatum's case was a big deal for a minute and a half before it was determined you didn't have anything to do with it. Someone tipped them off the second Colorado showed up in town. It wasn't long after he left that the interest fizzled out." I knew how that worked all too well. "Boyfriend kills girlfriend is nowhere near as juicy as best friend kills best friend in black magic ritual while in a jealous, lesbian rage. Or some shit," he said and planted his hands on his hips. "Look, she let it go and didn't send the cops out for you."

"You are the cops."

"Ha, yeah, I'm also your estranged fiancé." Dominika looked at Cyrus and mouthed fiancé. "You were in that bed, dead as far as the world knew, and I was right there with you. Who the fuck do you think would take the rap for that should we get caught?"

He had a point. "Fine. But at no point am I telling my mother you and I are married." Mike swallowed hard and clenched his teeth. "I'm sorry, but planning a wedding seems a little ridiculous right now."

"All right, shut up," Lupe hissed, pinching her fingers together like a duck. "You two figure it out later. Right now, Dylan, *mija*, take care of your mother and the memory of your friend. That isn't going anywhere." Lupe pointed to the center of my chest with a weathered finger then ran a heavy, warm hand over my shoulder to my elbow. The motion was odd and out of place. "*Liberación*."

"What?" I looked down my arm at her. My weird tattoo hadn't budged in my trip, and I worried it never would. I opened my mouth to ask about it but was cut off by strangely over-attentive people.

Cyrus clapped his hands together and smiled tightly. "Well, let's get you home."

"Finally." Dominika rolled her eyes reminding me of a bitchy teenager.

"Dylan, I'll come back for your car later." Mike reached a caring arm out to me. "You're probably ready to get into your own clothes." His nostrils flared, and he bit the inside of his lip. "Come on."

"Take a few days to rest with your family." Lupe patted me kindly on the hand.

Mike's arm wrapped around my shoulders as he escorted me to the front door. Keys in hand, he seemed all too eager to rush me out of the house. All of them were acting as though I'd just been diagnosed with cancer, but nobody wanted to break the news.

The moments passed too quickly. Before I knew it, I was sliding into the passenger seat of Mike's SUV. He reached over the top of me to buckle my belt.

"I'm not an invalid." I batted him off and buckled myself.

Cyrus stood on the porch, waving with an eerie aura of faux happiness. Long legs showcased in perfectly pressed black slacks, his height was nothing next to Dominika who stood more than an inch taller in stilettos. The November weather kicked up leaves around the porch and up the steps. Lupe's stump echoed against the wood slats as she joined the gang for the last big goodbye. Squinting my eyes against the scene, I seriously questioned my sanity. And partly theirs.

"We'll call you," Mike yelled over the top of the SUV to the weirdos on the porch.

Cyrus held a thumb up at me and then stuck his hands in his pockets, looking down sheepishly at shiny brown shoes. The engine roared to life. Cyrus's perfect green eyes looked up at me through thick lashes without lifting his head. Lupe waved slightly, and Dominika appeared otherwise unamused. But Cyrus took those last few moments, before we turned and lost sight of each other, to look at me as though it may have been the last time he would see me. His eyes locked on to mine, brows raised. An out of place swaggering smile spread across his face a moment before Mike turned the wheel and headed down the drive.

Frantically, I checked the mirror. The three had turned away, and only their shadows could be seen on the porch as they disappeared inside, and I moved further and further away.

What the fuck did that mean? Had it meant anything? Had there even been a look?

I turned my body and looked out the large back window for any sign of distress coming from the house. The sun shone brightly on its white slatted siding, appearing completely unassuming considering the devilish thing that had occurred there.

"You okay?" Mike asked, running a hand over my thigh. He stopped the car at the end of the driveway and looked at me. Sparkling blue-green eyes studied my face as he bit his lip.

No. I am far from okay. So far, in fact, I don't think I'll ever come back from not fucking okay.

Heart thudding in my chest, I swallowed hard. "Fine." I cleared my throat and nodded. "I'm fine." My eyes darted out the back window at the house I could hardly see.

Liar, liar, pants on fire.

THREE

"TAHOE?" I ASKED MIKE AS WE TURNED ONTO MY MOM'S street. It was the first thing I'd said on the awkward twenty-minute drive, and he jumped slightly at the unexpected sound of my voice.

He cleared his throat. "Yeah. Tahoe." I looked at the side of his head, not even having to ask. "It was the first thing that came to mind."

"We've never been to Tahoe," I pointed out.

"And? It was all I had." He put the SUV in park in front of my mom's. "You don't have to lie." The radio stopped when he turned the key and pulled it out. "The weather was beautiful. You rested for three days. Drinking craft beer and eating fancy cheese."

"Really?" The idea was laughable. Although, I did love

beer. And cheese.

"You're a millennial. Isn't that what you're supposed to do in your downtime?"

I opened my mouth to say something bitchy but stopped myself. "I'm lucky to be alive. I don't do downtime anymore."

"Touché." Opening his door, he stopped and looked at me. "I'm ready for downtime when you're ready for downtime."

I knew that already, but his reminder brought out guilt I thought I'd squashed during my trip to the hothouse. He'd never understood the fact that we weren't a thing anymore and completely squashed any boundaries that entailed. The only difference in that moment was me and my promises. At some point, I'd have to make good on those promises and let go of all the occult bullshit for his sake. The poor boy really wasn't cut out for it.

Letting out a breath, I knocked on the front door. Bright sunlight glinted through the thick tree on the front lawn, and I squinted against it. Leaves fell to the grass in swirling spirals. Wind kicked up my thick, wavy ponytail and blew it over my face. I swiped it away, blowing at tiny hairs that had landed across my mouth and stuck to my lips.

The door opened, and she was already talking. "Dylan, there you are." Mom reached thick arms out to me. "I was so worried about you."

"Hey, Mom," Mike said over my shoulder. Mom lifted a hand from my back to grab his hand. One big happy family. "Told you she was alive."

I scoffed. I couldn't help it. "As much as I'm enjoying this love sandwich, can I be released?"

Mom moved into the house and out of our way. It had been too long since I'd been home. My real home. The one I'd pumped full of lead. Walking into my mom's house made me feel like I *was* home. I'd need to get my things from my apartment eventually. I hadn't written a sentence in weeks and had nothing on the back burner to get me by. Money was quickly becoming top priority over demons and dead things. Moving back home seemed the most appropriate choice.

"You hungry?" Mom asked, disappearing into the kitchen.

I smiled and looked back at Mike. "Yes." The action was more flirtatious than I'd anticipated and a self-assured smile spread over Mike's face. Surprised at my own boldness, I turned away quickly and followed Mom to the kitchen.

"How was Tahoe?" she asked, rummaging through the fridge. "Beer?" She handed one to Mike but didn't offer me one.

"Thanks, Mom. I'd love a beer," I said sarcastically.

"I'm sorry I wasn't sure...." She let the sentence trail off and reached into the fridge to pull out another cold bottle.

"Weren't sure about what?" I looked at Mike scornfully then back at my mom again. "About what?" I pushed.

"Dylan, I had to explain to your mom the situation." I glared at him. "After Detective Colorado left, the drinking." His eyes burrowed into mine and he raised his brows. Shrugging gently, he added, "I couldn't leave her in the dark as to why I took you out of town for the weekend."

My jaw set tight, I pulled a calming breath through my nose. "Yes. Of course. The drinking." I didn't bother covering up the disdain in my voice. Tahoe and binge drinking. Excellent choice of excuse. "I'm okay now, Mom," I said, my tone reassuring. "Just had a hard time with it all and needed a vacation."

Mike coughed up beer and nearly spit it out at my ironic choice of words. "There's still a lot to do, but we're back now." He laid a heavy hand on my shoulder and gave it a squeeze. "I'll be here too. Soon enough, it'll all be over."

I offered a tight smile and then swigged my glorious beer. It felt like I'd been living in a nightmare from which I couldn't wake. Mike's assumption it would all be over pulled at something in my gut. Something that said he was dead wrong. A part of me, the part that reminded me I was pushing thirty and too damn old for that shit, wished it were true. If only having Mike hanging over my shoulder all the time was the cure to what ailed me.

My dead best friend hadn't popped up in the hours I'd been back with the living. No dead things scurried along the ceiling or stumbled down the hall. With the exception of the random power surge and auditory hallucination, of course. I drank to the hope my life was on the mend, and soon it would all be over. I could go back to fucking things up without the influence of the occult.

I tossed the dark brown beer bottle into the recycling bin next to the sink, and it crashed into the pile of empties at the bottom. I peered in to see it was mostly full. Mom had pounded a few back in my absence. She was no teetotaler, but she had cut back on the drinking after Dad was killed. By the looks of it, she'd killed at least a twelve pack and was working on another.

A bin full of empties. Thanks for the passive-aggressive guilt trip, Mom.

Mike moved behind me and tossed his bottle in too. Silently,

I pointed to the bin. Our eyes met, and he raised an inquisitive brow. He knew Mom almost as well as I did. She'd taken him on as a son long before I even admitted he was my boyfriend. He knew just as well as I did what that mostly full bin meant. I needed to get my shit together before Mom killed her liver.

Later, while we ate the delicious lunch Mom had prepared on the fly, I broke the silence abruptly and interrupted his chewing. "Will you help me get my apartment in order tomorrow?" I asked Mike.

Nodding, one cheek filled with food as he noshed it all down. "Yeah," he said, swallowing the lump that had filled his mouth. "There are a few things you should probably do tomorrow."

Shooting him an evil glare, I assumed he meant sex.

He dropped his chin and looked at me under his brows. "Love, we have to work out the funeral arrangements." His condescending tone allowed my embarrassment to fade quickly and make way for cynicism.

"That's *exactly* what I want to do. Plan my best friend's funeral." My bacon, *bacon*, tomato sandwich abruptly lost all appeal, and I shoved it away.

He laid his sandwich down gently on the plate and leaned toward me. "Trust me when I say I'd rather have you bent over this dining table tomorrow than plan Tatum's funeral, but these are the cards we were dealt."

My breath caught in my throat. The mental image of he and I flashed in my mind and pulled the muscles tight in my core. Thankful Mom had left us to eat alone while she puttered around the house pretending not to be listening in, I used her to stick a jab at his crude remark. "Well," I scoffed arrogantly and folded my arms over my chest, "who's the freak wanting to bang on his mother's dining table?"

"Funny." He shoved half his sandwich in his food hole, staring at me the whole time. The muscles in his jaw flexed vigorously as he attempted to chew his massive bite. "She's not my mother," he said around bread and bacon.

"Might as well be." I stood and walked my plate to the sink. My half-eaten sandwich looked mostly pathetic on my plate. Pulling out a strip of bacon, I sat the plate on the counter next to the sink. "Look," I said, shoving the bacon into my mouth. "I know you're trying to help." Admittedly, I was still torn on whether or not I wanted his help. "And I appreciate it—"

"But fuck off?" he butted in, sorrow in his voice.

Hands gripping the edge of the sink, I shook my head. Wherever I had been going with that sentence didn't matter in the long run. Chuckling to myself at the ridiculousness of my own thoughts, I decided to let it go. There was nothing I could say that would stop him from trying to rescue me. Knowing Michael Petersen, he'd die trying to save me from myself.

"You said but fuck," I teased under my breath. Another piece of bacon was salvaged from the sandwich, and I shoved it in with its delicious fallen brethren. Mike laughed at my joke and the mood lightened instantly. "Forget it." Last piece of bacon, in the gullet. "Thank you for not giving up on me. I'm glad it's not me heading for a piney box."

An exaggerated sigh of relief pushed loudly through Mike's pursed lips. Grateful I didn't pull him through the ringer again, he finished the last few bites of his sandwich in peaceful silence.

Knowing him like I did, the moment was just one step closer to *his* normal.

“What are you going to do about that?” He pointed to the bin as he washed his plate.

I shrugged. “Nothing.” He looked hurt. “She’s an adult. Also, hopefully, her daughter won’t be running for her life and fending off the forces of evil driving her to drink anymore,” I whispered over the running water.

“You know there’s only one sure way to make absolutely certain that never happens.” He turned off the sink and stared at the side of my head. I refused to look at him. I knew what he was going to say, and I really didn’t know how I felt about it.

“Do you really think cutting Cyrus out of my life is going to suddenly solve everything?

“No, but I do know he’s at the center of a shit storm, and if I were you, I’d be steering clear of it. Besides, that was Tatum’s world. She’s the one who got you involved in all of that. Got you hooked up with,” he stopped and lowered his voice, “Vampires and shit. Malcolm’s gone. Tatum’s gone. All the bad guys are gone. The mystery is solved.”

“Weren’t you just saying there were new dead girls to worry about?”

“Hey, as far as my precinct is concerned, Sam and Philippe are responsible for the deaths of those prostitutes. Regina’s death wouldn’t be a stretch. I could close it up and never worry about it again.”

“And the new bodies?” I asked cautiously.

“Like you said, Kool-Aid.”

“Mike, they’re being decapitated. That’s not something you

can do to yourself."

He folded thick arms over his broad chest. "I thought you didn't care?"

"I don't. But that doesn't mean I don't want you to. You're a detective, detect. Or don't. But don't let a murderer go free because you want to make my life easier. If I'm being totally honest with myself, I'd like to see the true faces behind the crimes. Are they like Sam and fake-ass Philippe? Losers with a Lestat complex. Were they coerced into it by Azelie and Zoran? Marienne and the House of Porte, are they the only cabal on the hunt for miracle blood? My curiosity won't let this go. No matter what I say."

He nodded. "I'll make you a deal. Let's get through this week and I'll check on the cases, see where everyone's at. The least I can do is keep up-to-date and make sure they're all even related."

I really couldn't force him to do anything. If he gave a little, I'd give a little. "Deal."

"But first, you need a break from life. If only to keep from keeling over in your mom's kitchen."

"It's four in the afternoon, what am I supposed to do for the next twelve plus hours?"

He shrugged thick shoulders and stepped closer to me. "Watch *Jeopardy* with your mom. Wash your hair. Put on your own clothes. I don't know, just be normal for a while. Tomorrow, we'll take care of everything."

His cologne filled the space between us. "And what will you be doing while I'm being normal?"

"Working." His masculine fingers played over a strand of

loose hair and tucked it behind my ear. "I've spent the last three days with a dead girl. I missed some stuff."

A flush brought red to my cheeks. Clearing my throat, I forced myself to look away from his gaze. "Too bad." A growl of hunger rolled through my chest.

Chuckling softly, Mike ran his hand down the curve of my back. "There is nothing I want more than to stay here with you." He tenderly touched his lips to my forehead. "I'll see you as soon as it's possible."

"What's so damn important right now anyway?" I was legitimately jealous of his job for the first time ever.

"Dead people." He tugged on my ponytail. "You seem to be on the mend. You've even started hitting on me again. I better duck out now before you notice what you're doing and stop."

I let out a long, contented laugh. "I don't know what I am, but I know I'm not dead, which seems to be a requirement for your attention at the moment." Wrapping my hand around his strong forearm, I looked him in the eyes. "Looks like I lose. Go save someone."

"Back from hell but still unchanged. You laughed during *Bambi* didn't you?"

"Go on now." I pushed lightly on his chest, backing him out of the kitchen.

"You did, didn't you?" At the door, he stopped and held on to the jamb. "Other women your age are planning baby showers and hunting for Mr. Right on the internet. You're shoving a man out of your house because you'd rather he spend time with dead people than make you blush. You really always have been one of a kind. One hundred percent impossible."

If it walks like a duck.

I let out an exacerbated sigh. "Just because I'm not falling down weeping at every diaper commercial, or dead girl shambling through my apartment, doesn't mean I'm callous. It just means I'm reasonable and independent. Live with it or don't, I'm so past worrying about that kind of shit I can't come close to explaining it to you. And… as for Mr. Right… there's no point in hunting, is there?" It slipped out before I could stop it. Subconsciously, I knew it to be true. I was and would always be Mike's girl. Might as well just start rolling with it. The slightest hint of a smile ticked at the corners of his mouth. "Get your ass off my front porch before I have to call the cops."

"Ha, ha, ho, you better stay put tonight, missy." He tapped the tip of my nose. "Or I'll have to put you in cuffs." Stealing a kiss, he turned and sauntered happily down the walk.

"That better be a promise," I said under my breath, shutting the door.

I couldn't have been more grateful the door was already shut when the hunger growled again, rumbling ominously through my chest and bubbling up my throat. After a pack of salami and multiple strips of fried bacon, I didn't think my three-day-dead heart could handle any more meat, but my mouth watered for it.

"Well, what are your plans tonight?" Mom asked from the living room.

Stomach rumbling, I shuffled into the living room. "I'm just gonna go take a shower and wash my hair. I feel like hell." *Literally.*

"Tahoe didn't help?" Her hopeful expression waned on my rocky feelings for Mike.

"We're okay, Mom," I reassured her without making a fuss about it. "No promises, but I'm trying. 'Kay?" I knew in my heart I would be *trying* in one way or another until the day I finally croaked.

Do or do not. There is no try.

"And Tatum?" Her voice quivered.

Letting out a long breath, I tucked my hands into the oversized pockets of Mike's sweatpants. "One day at a time."

"Yeah." She nodded. "We'll make sure her service is perfect." Her eyes glistened.

A half-hearted forced smile pulled one side of my mouth up. "Thanks."

"Get some rest," she called out to me as I made my way down the hall.

The moment my eyes fell on my bed the idea of washing my hair was out the window. Getting out of Mike's baggy, comfortable clothes was the last thing I wanted to do. If only my own girly clothes fit like that and had pockets. I made a note to start shopping in the men's section as I dug into the back of my top drawer. Right where I'd left it, my little wooden box.

Green and probably too ancient to be healthy, the last hairy bud I had stashed away waited for me. I stuffed a towel under the door to block the smoke and opened the window. Crisp November air wafted through the room. I lit a cigarette from the pack I had stashed with the box and let it burn while I hit the pipe. Blowing the smoke out the window, I inhaled deeply and let the drug take effect.

When the weed and the cigarette were ash, I snuffed them in the toilet and lay down on the bed. After days dead, I wasn't in any mood to sleep, but I didn't doubt the weed would soon ensure I drifted off into peaceful slumber.

A quick eyeball search of the bed and nightstand didn't turn up the TV remote. Too lazy to move from my spot, I decided to forego TV Land for the night. Andy Griffith wasn't worth the scramble off the bed to hunt for the remote. Light from the bathroom illuminated the dark room well enough to make out every shape I already knew by heart anyway.

The day had passed without incident, barring my bathtub delusion, and it did seem as though I'd cured myself. No shiny black demon stalked me home. No skeleton-faced Mike to frighten me into kicking him out to save his life. No spectral best friend jabbering in my ear. Nothing but me and my undying need to push people away. Normal. Why couldn't I just be normal?

Because normal was boring. Normal meant conforming to someone else's standard of living. In my case, that was usually Mike's standards. It meant no Cyrus. No demons, no Lupe, no running for my life. Just me and Mom and Mike, forever. Or, until I died. Which judging by my recent life choices could have been any time or place. I just hoped my afterlife held more for me than my made-up hell and the demon disguised as my best friend.

With visions of Mike and babies and walk-in closets dancing in my head, my eyes fluttered closed, sleep imminent. Morning would bring with it real troubles, human life and death troubles, I couldn't avoid no matter how badly I wanted to. Tatum was dead and gone—for all I knew. Seemingly cured of my curses, the next step toward finding myself again was burying the thorn in my side and putting her to rest for good.

I prayed to a God I didn't know I believed in and begged that she was in a good place. A place better than the shithole we called Earth. Away from assholes like Azelie and Marienne, and me for that matter. I wanted nothing more than to know, not hope or believe, *know* she was happy.

I drifted into silence thinking about Tatum, sleep tickling the edges, the world humming into the background.

"Marco," a familiar voice flittered in with the wind from far out in the ether.

Polo.

FOUR

I SAT AWAKE FOR AN HOUR WAITING FOR HER, BUT LIKE Dad's delusional visit, nothing more came of it. Worrying the voice I'd heard was the embodiment of my black demon, I slipped the Devil's Trap over my head for good measure. For whatever it was worth, I held it out in front of me like a shield and threatened the son of a bitch within an inch of its life.

Hardly moving my lips, I whispered, so as to not wake up Mom, "Tatum, are you there?"

It became apparent I'd crossed a few wires on my trip back from hell—the otherworld, whatever the fuck they wanted to call it—when minutes passed and nothing came scurrying out from the shadows. Cyrus and Lupe could sugarcoat it with fancy words, but I knew what that place was. Hell. Pure and simple.

With no additional peep from my dead best friend and unable to fight sleep anymore, my eyes closed again. Between the pot and my *vacation* to the *otherworld*, I figured minor auditory hallucinations weren't off the chart for side effects. Dreamless sleep came and took me away quietly.

Morning brought with it a bright new day and an annoying bird. Grumbling, I tossed over in the bed, pulling the blanket higher to cover my head. My toes poked from the edge of the blanket, instantly cool. Had the sun not been shining through the slit in the curtain, I'd have been nervous to leave my tootsies exposed to the dark. But the bird chirped on, reminding me the night had faded away, and I shoved my head under the pillows. Muffled singing penetrated the poly-fill, but I closed my eyes against the disruption.

Alone in the darkened solitude of my pillow, I held my eyes closed tight. I wanted to drift off into silent sleep again. No dreams had clouded my slumber. No nightmares kept me running all night. But I wasn't restored. Sleep had been silent, but not restful. And though I couldn't recall anything specific, I knew my mind hadn't rested.

I took a moment to allow the darkness a chance to pull me back in. The bird's chirping subdued by thick billows of cotton, I began to give way to sleep. Breathing slowed, fingertips grown numb, and the world faded away.

Something rough brushed against my exposed toes.

Did that just happen?

My heart stopped. It had been just a moment, just a slight sensation, but adrenaline surged, and my eyes popped open. I couldn't be sure it was nothing. Not completely. I waited a few long moments, listening for any sound, waiting for another touch. Nothing.

I breathed through pursed lips and closed my eyes again. My three-day-dead brain truly wasn't to be trusted. I pulled my feet higher under the fluffy blanket, the very tips of my toes left out to feel the cool air.

Clicking. *Tick, tick, tick.* A scurry. Something hot tapped my toes.

I gasped quietly from beneath the pillow. *That happened.* There was no denying it. I was wide awake and focused on the foot in question. Blood raced through my veins as adrenaline took hold of my nervous system. Experience told me if I lifted the pillow to look, there would be something scary waiting for me. In my mind, a shiny black demon stood at the foot of my bed tickling my toes with the tips of his claw-like fingers.

Flight-or-fight fear coursing through me, I gathered every last ounce of courage I had. Focusing my energy on the space around my legs, I imagined where the thing was standing. The sensation of another body in the space tangled with my aura. I closed my eyes, gritted my teeth, and let my barefoot fly, kicking hard toward the foot of the bed with a grunt.

Contact.

"Oomph," a man groaned.

Using up the last of my adrenaline, I flung the pillow away and sat up to face my intruder.

A guttural scream tore at my throat. "You scared the fuck out of me," I wailed and threw a pillow at Mike.

"You kicked me in the mouth," he said, holding his lip.

"What the fuck was your mouth doing by my foot?"

He sighed. "It wasn't by your foot. I was leaning over the end of the bed when you kicked me." His tone insinuated I was to blame.

Expression flat, I stared at him blankly. "I'm not sure I really want to know what you were scheming." Instinctively, I sat up on my knees and scooted to the edge of the bed. "You're bleeding." I pointed to his lip. A red gash in the center of his bottom lip leaked a drip of blood.

"Ugh." He pulled his brows together and looked at me disapprovingly.

Unconsciously, I focused on the blood. His full bottom lip swelled from the injury. He licked at the gash, swiping away blood momentarily before it oozed out again. Moving to my knees, I scurried toward him. I wrapped one strong hand around the back of his head and pulled his mouth to mine. My wet tongue moved across his swollen lip and pulled his blood into my mouth. A shaky breath pushed through his stunned lips.

Coppery tang tingled my tongue. Rolling hunger tightened my stomach. I hadn't planned it, but on instinct, I knelt at the foot of my bed and sucked the blood from his lip. Mike's breathing came fast and hard, and in a heartbeat, his arms were wrapped around me. The blood was gone, but he wasn't. His mouth pressed hard against mine and I did well to stay upright on my knees. The taste of blood filled my mouth and ran a feral appetite through my body.

Manly hands pressed tight to my back and held me against his chest. My uncontained boobs pressed into him and I thought for a moment about the pajamas I'd worn. With the copper flavor completely faded as the blood clotted, his usual minty taste took over. The ravenous sensation that had churned soul-deep left as quickly as it had appeared and in its wake, an entirely new need roared through my core.

"Pancakes?" Mom knocked on the door but didn't bother waiting before opening it. "Oh."

Her eyes went wide, and I shoved Mike away like we should have been studying instead of making out. Without another word, she shut the door. Mike stood with his hands on his head, face set to stunned, chest heaving underweighted breaths.

A sudden sense of shame filled me, and I blushed at what I'd done and could hardly meet his eyes. Being a notorious bitch didn't automatically make me a tiger in the sack. Though, I thought, it might be time soon to make that an option. Life was becoming shorter by the day, and I'd yet to fully unleash my inner minx. Sober, anyway.

"Sorry," I said quietly.

His brows pulled together, he moved his hands from his head to his hips. "I don't want an apology. Ever. At some point, an explanation would be nice. But right now, I have a serious boner and I gotta pee." His face looked pained.

"Go pee then." I shooed him away.

"That really wasn't the answer I was shooting for." He grumbled and went to the bathroom.

"Pancakes," I said excitedly and pointed toward the kitchen.

"Yeah." More grumbling and a ludicrously long piss.

Mom hustled through the kitchen, pancakes in the making. From hell to pancakes. Never a dull moment in the life of Dylan Hart.

“So…” I started, rocking forward on my toes. “Got any bacon?”

“You’re gonna turn into bacon,” Mom said, looking over her shoulder at me.

I slapped my chunky butt. “Too late.”

Mike’s laugh was deep and throaty, full of things not appropriate for conversations with Mom. “I’ll get you some bacon frying,” she said, ignoring Mike’s unspoken innuendo, cheeks flushed pink from embarrassment.

Mike leaned in close over my shoulder. “Has she ever cooked this much in a row?”

Curling my lip in thought, I shrugged. “Not really. She was more of a microwave dinner kind of mom.” Guilt? Nerves? Whatever the reason, I was happy to be the recipient to Mom’s newfound Martha Stewart.

“Nutritious.”

“I didn’t acquire this ass on accident.” I nodded in the direction of the culprit, Mom’s equally chunky trunk and the thick slabs of pork belly she dropped into the hot pan.

The bacon was everything I’d hoped it would be and the pancakes killed the sweet tooth I’d developed overnight. The hunger I’d felt with Mike was gone, and I was honestly starting to feel—*relatively*—normal again.

“Wanna change out of your jammies so we can hit the road. Sorry to say, you’ve got a busy day. Ha, see what I did there?” Smiling smugly at his rhyme, he pointed at his baggy clothes I was still wearing.

“Yeah. Clever.” I looked down at the faded Pixies shirt and sweats I’d slept in. Seeming to revel in the idea I’d slept in his clothes, Mike was left at the table smiling smugly all by his lonesome when I ditched him to change out of my jammies.

Mike pulled his ginormous vehicle to the curb after an uncomfortably silent car ride. The monstrosity blocked most of the driveway at the head of the garage, above which I lived. CA Exempt plates pretty much allowed him free parking anywhere, or so he boasted, so the usual lack of parking on my street was a non-issue.

Incessant barking from the fleabag over the fence welcomed me home. Mr. Garabedian stood on the curb, sweeping fallen leaves into a pile. His stern expression weighed heavily on me, and I timidly met his eyes. Mr. Garabedian was one of the only people on the planet who made me feel like I was six years old.

"Miss Hart," his gruff voice crooned. He scowled at Mike's parking job, eyed the plates and seemed to let the matter go before making a fuss.

"Hi, Mr. Garabedian."

"Fixed your door," he grumbled as he jutted an ancient thumb at my apartment.

"Thank you."

"What'ya doing up there breaking a hole the size of a—"

"Dog," Mike said quickly. "A big one. Chased her home and busted into her door when she slammed it on it." The sound of the dog barking in the background made the moment more tangible than it ever could've been.

He shook his head, loose, wrinkled jowls shaking with it. "Ah, well, no dogs allowed."

"No, you see, it wasn't *my* dog. It was—"

"Eh," he waved me off, "you're too loud. Your rent is late. And you always park in the shade. Consider this your thirty-day notice."

Boldly, I stepped closer to the old man. "Consider this fuck you." I shoved past him and trotted up the stairs, Mike snickering behind me. "You don't own the shade, asshole," I grumbled under my breath.

"One day, your mouth is going to get you into more shit than you're prepared for," Mr. Garabedian barked in a manner far different than the dog.

"Too late." The new door came equipped with a new lock and the key Mr. Garabedian had kindly left sticking out of the deadbolt for safe keeping. "What a dick." That key had to have been jammed in the lock unattended for a week.

The key turned over smoothly and the door opened with ease. Angels sang from the heavens and a glowing light illuminated from the jamb. Sort of. Reveling for a moment in the free-moving door, I pouted at the idea that door wasn't *my* door. Someone else would have the luxury I'd always hoped for. All it took was a voodoo curse and something drudged up from hell to make it happen.

The apartment looked the same. Musty and eerily empty. Small bullet holes dotted the wall in the hallway. A vivid memory of gunshots rang in my head. I blinked against the sound and caught my breath.

"You okay?" Mike's heavy hand fell on my shoulder.

"Yeah." I cleared my throat. "Yeah. Fine. Just weird being back here. Feels like an eternity." I trailed off and focused on the details of my apartment. Bits of wood from the splintered door stuck out of the carpet. The stale smell of uncirculated air clung to my nose.

"Well, I'm all yours today. So where do you want to start?"

"Uh, I don't know." The last time I moved I'd packed and split while he was at work. "I hadn't really thought about it." A shuffling sound pulled my attention to the hallway. "We don't have any boxes," I said, absent from the conversation.

"I figured we wouldn't get it all done today anyway so I didn't bother hunting anything down. You still have those suitcases we bought, right?" I nodded, focused on the hallway, waiting for the sound to come again. "Just pack those with stuff you're taking to your mom's, then we'll come back for the rest after—" He stopped short.

"Good plan." Shuffling echoed through the hallway again. "Did you… hear that?" Brows tight together, I left Mike to investigate the noise. Having recently returned from the dead, mysterious shuffling was low on my fear list and high on the kill-the-fuck-out-of-it list. Although, I'd left my gun at Sween during my swift exit, so killing the fuck out of it would require some ingenuity.

The lights were off, and the blinds closed in the back of the apartment. Shadows fell over objects I hardly recognized. The space felt odd, almost foreign. I'd been away too long.

As I moved into my room, another phantom gunshot rang out. Flinching against the sound, my hands instinctively flew up to protect my face. My ears buzzed and I clamped my hands over them.

"Dylan?" Mike stomped through the hallway toward me. "What the hell?"

Certain I looked like an asshole standing there holding my ears, I dropped my arms quickly to my sides. "Nothing. Just weird being back," I repeated, chest heaving, heart thudding.

Distrustfully, he furrowed his brow. "Yeah. I'm sure. Honestly, I'm glad you're leaving this place. The landlord is a dick."

I sighed. "Not always. He's just old and particular. Most of the time I don't even see him."

"You're defending that guy?"

I shook my head. "No. Just trying to cope with life and living without being a total cuntbag." *And failing miserably.*

Mike blinked a few times. "Well, I guess that's one for the pro column."

Appeasing him, I flashed a half-grin and moved into the bedroom. "All I really need right now is clothes and daily stuff. We can come back for the rest after the funeral." I stopped fast. *Funeral.* It'd slid right out of my mouth like nothing. Like I was talking about needing milk. My lungs stopped working for what felt like a full, agonizing minute. "It's not really all that important." *Compared to other things.*

I considered my growing collection of Halloween PEZ dispensers and beelined for the shelf to ensure they made the move safely. Some things really *were* that important.

With no boxes handy and no drive to hunt any down, we were stuck using whatever luggage I had laying around. Two rolling do-dads, a couple of duffle motherfuckers, and a gaggle of two-severed-heads-sized totes made up my moving-back-home equipment.

Between the two of us, it took less than a few hours to pack up the majority of my house. In all honesty, I didn't own much. All my clothes, shoes, toiletries, and miscellaneous memorabilia I couldn't live without took up most of the bags. I packed books, DVDs, and a healthy CD collection in a few of the leftover totes. The last I filled with important papers, bills—mostly all unpaid—and the like. Furniture and any last big shit would have to wait until I had more time. My life sat in a jumble of bags and suitcases in the middle of the living room.

"I have to say," Mike said, standing back and looking at the pile of random outdated luggage. "This is the most haphazard collection of moving boxes I've ever had the pleasure of hefting into my vehicle."

Between numerous college buddies and the divorce rate among police officers, I was sure this wasn't the first move he'd assisted in.

"Thanks for..." *helping me escape the terror that has become my life,* "loaning me your muscle and your vehicle."

"Eh, you know." He waved me off. "It's not like I had a lot to do on a Tuesday. After a week vacation. During a high-profile murder investigation."

I thanked him with a punch to the arm and shoved a bag into his chest. "Let's get the fuck out of here. I'm hungry."

He collected a few smaller bags from the pile. "That trip to the otherworld kicked your beefcake into overdrive."

"Ha. No shit." I hefted a bag on my shoulder and leaned an overly stuffed duffle bag against my chest. "Move it. I'm serious."

Mike boldly conquered the steps, beefy arms loaded with my shit. I followed carefully behind. Bravely managing one concrete step at a time. Eyeing the you'll-poke-your-eye-out branch only steps ahead, I quickly developed a plan for working around it with my arms full. It'd grown more dangerous points in the week I hadn't seen it. Yellowing leaves dangled from spindly branches and even more decaying, slimy leaves were scattered across the already treacherous steps. Moving closer to the slat-siding of the garage that butted up to one side of the staircase, I used the duffle bag to push the branch away from me enough to squeeze by. A leaf popped off a branch and landed on the bag. The branch moved easily, and I slid by with nothing more than a yellowing stowaway. As I passed, the branch slid across the bag and snapped back into place sending dying leaves flying over me and the steps.

"Damn it," I groaned, leaves jutting from my unruly ponytail.

By the last step, my legs were screaming at me. It'd been too long since I'd maneuvered that staircase and I was paying the price.

"I could've gotten those." Mike took the bags from me.

Hands free, I shook the leaves from my fluffy ponytail. Just another day in paradise. I knew one thing for sure, I wasn't going to miss that fucking apartment and the nonsense it brought with it. I would, however, miss alone time. I dug the last twig out of my puff of hair. Something rustled in Mr. Garabedian's garage.

"You could've," I said absently, focused on the scratching sound.

Mike shoved the duffle bag in the back of his SUV. "You okay?"

"What the hell is that?" I asked, standing on tiptoes to see into the tiny windows in the garage door.

"What?"

"That scratching."

Too short to see, I gave up. I almost asked Mike to take a peek. He already thought I was losing it; shining a light on the fact was probably not in my best interest. If Tatum had been there, I'd have asked her. The thought of her brought bile up my throat. I hadn't just lost a friend. I'd killed her. And with her my own soul. My threshold for sanity was quickly waning.

Two bags slung over my shoulder and the handle of a small rolling bag in my hand, I shut the door for the last time. It closed with ease, and the lock slid over without a fuss. The damn thing had been a thorn in my side for a year and the day I move out was the day I didn't have to fight it. If that wasn't indicative of my life, I didn't know what was.

The dog barked a final farewell from his side of the fence. I shot him a cocked grin and expertly held the tree limb with my free hand to steady it and save myself from a second leaf rain. Of all the times I'd fought that damn thing, it took a trip to hell to turn things in my favor.

When I cleared the last step, Mike pulled his top half from the ass end of his SUV and asked, "Is that the last of it?"

"Yup." I shoved the rolling bag into the seat. "You will come help me move my couch and shit, right?" My stomach tightened at both the thought of having to ask and the possibility of him saying no.

A meaty hand ran over his naturally wavy hair. He must've missed his latest trip to the barber—it fell over the tops of his ears. "Of course. But, I gotta ask, where am I moving it to?"

I stared at him from under furrowed brows. While I was

ready to work on *us*, working on it and living together did not live in the same zip code. "It doesn't really match your décor."

"I don't mean my place, jackass." He paused, seeming to search for the best words. "Tatum's house is technically yours."

My jaw dropped. Literally hit my chest. "I can't believe you even suggested that."

"You lived there when we met. I didn't think—"

"It's fine. Forget it." I spun on my heel and headed for the passenger door. "You know what—" I stopped, "It's not fine. It's not fucking fine at all." I turned to face him, eyes glistening. "I killed her," I said, my voice echoing through the neighborhood. "I killed my only friend. She's gone and it's because of me." He opened his mouth to interrupt. "No." I stuck my hand up at him. "I did. There's no arguing it. There is nothing in this world that will make me live in that house now. Nothing."

Over his shoulder, the glimmer of a shambling headless corpse came into view. My breath caught in my throat.

Not again.

"I'm sorry. I didn't mean—"

My mouth hung open. Breathing was a memory. Something I thought perhaps I'd dreamt. I shook my head, waking up my lungs. I blinked away the vision and promised myself it was a hallucination as a result of major trauma. "Mike." I shifted my eyes up at him. "Can you make sure I turned everything off?" I asked suddenly. "Please," I added for effect, still mostly focused at the space over his shoulder.

Suspicion swept over him. He searched my eyes. I didn't dare glance over his shoulder. Didn't dare let on I was seeing things again. Eyes locked, he nodded. Without a word, he trotted up the stairs to meet my request.

I searched the street. The corpse was gone, but vining fear still crept through my limbs. I knew what I'd seen. I knew what I'd heard.

A breeze kicked up and whipped debris around my legs. The rustling of the leaves roused the dog that had been uncharacteristically quiet. His barking rang in my ears like breaking glass. Rage instantly bubbled up my gut.

Fuck that dog.

Fuck that tree.

Fuck this shithole.

A white flash from across the street pulled me out of my wrathful trance. The headless corpse had reappeared and was shuffling toward me. My legs were lead, glued to the spot. The narrow road allowed for quick passage from one side to the other, and in a blink, she was feet away. Purple hair bound her hands. She reached for me.

Regina.

The dog barked on but did nothing by way of headless zombie. I wanted to scream for Mike, but I knew if he didn't see what I was seeing, it was the loony bin for me. She could have reached out and touched me. If she had eyes, she probably would have.

Decaying fingers played through the air at me. I dodged twice before an uncontrollable scream pelted out from deep in my lungs. It was the first true scream I'd unleashed since it'd all began. In the grand scheme of things, the moment was mundane, but it was enough to kick me over that ledge.

My screams awakened in me a fire-hot rage that tore me

from my spot. Without thought, I hauled off in a run toward the stairs. Up the stairs was truly the best option for me. Either I wouldn't die alone, or someone sane could slap some sense into me. Either way, it meant salvation.

Half a dozen strides and I was at the stairs. I should have known better than to run. My toe caught the second step. Inertia shoved me forward, and I landed on my hands and knees against the concrete step. Regina stumbled onto the first step and grabbed hold of my foot. Her fingers were filthy. Had she been digging up graveyard dirt, too? I kicked and jerked, but her bound hands held firm. Gurgling black fluid bubbled at her stump. One hand on the banister for leverage, I shoved my foot into her chest. She stumbled back and lost her grip on my foot. I climbed to my feet and scurried up the stairs.

Halfway up the stairs, the tree limb. My limb. The limb of death. The fucking, piece of shit limb I'd been fighting for too damn long. Regina stepped up clumsily behind me. Oily liquid drizzled over her chest and down her boobs.

I'd escaped an untold hell dimension, and a headless dead bitch had sent me scrambling up a set of stairs I loathed more than Kanye West.

Ducking under the branch at the last second, I crawled up two steps and turned onto my butt. Regina, sightless, reached aimlessly for me. Thick blackness poured over her naked body from her stump.

I thought it was all over. I thought I'd stopped it all. I'd gone to hell. I'd killed the bad guy. All of them as far as I knew. More naked zombies were the last thing I'd expected.

"Fuck off, Regina."

I stood and grabbed hold of the limb, bowing it back toward me. Regina shambled up a step. Bullseye. Letting go of the branch sent it careening into the oily black stump atop her shoulders. Reaching out for me, the ghostly body burst into bits on impact and flittered away like ashes. Yellow leaves rained over the stairs. A few stuck to the oily rot she'd spattered on my feet. Leaves flipped through the air where a headless corpse had stood, intertwining with the dead bits and falling softly over my eyelashes. Instinctively, I flailed, batting at the floating pieces, waving them away as best I could. Heart thudding against my chest, I fell onto my butt, panting.

"What in the hell?" Mike bellowed, standing over the top of me.

I looked up over my head at Mike. His face, upside down, was a mix of fear and dread. As if the idea of me finally losing my shit terrified him more than me hacking off the heads of my enemies. Heavy breaths broke up my words. "Big… fucking… wasp." Mike quietly stared down at me. I whined and lay my head on the top step. "Gnarly fucker," I whispered.

"A wasp?"

I nodded and closed my eyes. My breath still ragged, I sigh. "Yup."

"You killed a wasp with your tree branch?"

Ironically… "I guess so."

"Okay." He ran his hand over his hair, refusing to look me in the eye. There was no doubt he suspected something was up. "Are you ready to roll?"

"Yes." I stood, nodding uncontrollably. "Can we get beer?" My hands shook, and I shoved them into my back pockets.

"And a steak?"

Mike laughed. "If that's all it takes to make you happy, I'll count myself lucky."

Adrenaline still pumping through my body, I stopped at the bottom of the stairs and planted a kiss on Mike that lasted longer than I'd anticipated.

"I should tell you," I started with dreamy, kiss-drunk eyes, "I have no money."

A tight knowing smile spread across his face as he nodded. "I figured."

I slid onto his supple leather seat. Mike shut the car door behind me and trotted around to his side. A sly smirk spread across my face when I caught him walking away in the side-view mirror. I shifted my gaze to see him from the driver's side. A pale glimmer followed. Not quite there, the form of a headless corpse stumbled behind him, desperate hands bound with black hair clawed at him. My stomach sank. I shook my head to rid myself of the vision. Mike opened the door and slid in.

He caught one glimpse of my face and asked, "What now?"

My breath had stopped. I stared over his shoulder at the gurgling black stump that stood outside his window. He looked over his shoulder at whatever I'd been staring at, seeing nothing. *Fuck*.

"Nothing. Why?" I gripped the armrest for dear life.

"Uh, you look like you're holding in buffet diarrhea."

"Specific," I squawked.

"It's the truth."

I shook my head. The stump pressed against the glass, streaking oily fluid over it with a morbid squeak. "Just need a beer."

Taking one last glance over his shoulder, he eyed me and started the engine and pulled away from the curb. Mr. Garabedian shuffled out of his door and watched us drive away. The corpse lumbered past him, rot- and grime-covered arms outstretched toward the car. He didn't look twice.

I'm a fucking nutcase.

FIVE

MIKE UNLOADED HIS SUV IN RECORD TIME. WE'D MADE tentative plans to grab lunch on the drive back, but I knew it wasn't a good idea. New shit had come to light, and I needed to get far away from the prying eyes and trigger finger of Michael Petersen. It wasn't him necessarily, but the naked headless dead bitches that seemed to be popping up left, right and center. Phantom white streaks had continued to catch my peripheral, driving me insane, and proving impossible to hide the anxiety they brought with them. He had been teetering on the edge of shipping me off to the nut farm as it was. I didn't need new kooky antics to solidify that line of thought.

When his phone rang while he was bringing in the last bag, I crossed my fingers it was work calling him in. He'd taken quite a bit of time off, so there was surely loads of work waiting for him. Avoiding Mike was all I had to fall back on until I could book it to Lupe and get to the bottom of the shambling corpse conundrum. Though the more I thought on it, Lupe's help was shoddy at best. She needed a disclaimer on her door: For entertainment purposes only.

"Damn it," he said to himself. I knew what that meant, and I let out a long relieved sigh. I had no idea how I was going to skate the fuzz otherwise. "Hey, I hate to ditch you, but I have to head to the station for a bit." He slid his phone back into his pocket. "Are you going to be okay?" he asked, standing at the front door.

I fought the urge to roll my eyes. *No*. No, I wasn't okay but telling him that would've been fucking stupid. "I'm fine. Really." Daylight was half over. I had an appointment with the funeral home at four, which I was sure I couldn't handle mentally, so Mike was a necessity, but for a while, I needed to be alone. If only to get a proper gauge on my level of sanity. "Go check in or whatever you have to do and meet me at the funeral home at four. I gotta shower and stuff."

Liar, liar, pants on fire.

"Just keep it together until I get there, please."

"Who do you think I am?" I asked sarcastically.

"Sometimes, I don't really know." His honesty stung deep, and I looked away from him. Moments of awkward silence crept on. Pointing to my shirt to call my attention, Mike flipped his finger under my nose, making a goofy sound. His joke reminded me of my dad, and I was flooded by a new wave of emotions.

"See you in a bit."

He leaned down and gave me a quick kiss on the forehead. The act came too easily to both of us and my natural urge to back away tugged at my muscles. I closed the door just in time to avoid the breakdown that had begun boiling inside me.

Knees trembling, I shook my father's face away from my memory and rubbed away the devil at my temples. "Mom," I called to her in the living room. "I need to borrow the car."

Mom's car was as ancient as her phone and chugged loudly down the crowded streets of East L.A. She didn't drive it much since she'd bought the truck, but it still ran like a champ. The tan leather interior, still in decent shape—give or take a cigarette burn or two—and supple with age, cradled my butt as I bounced over every pothole. The stale smell of smoke trapped for eternity in the vent systems mingled with another, familiar but unrecognizable, aroma that reminded me of elementary school and meeting Tatum for the first time. Mom had given her a ride home because her parents had forgotten to pick her up. It wasn't the last time that happened, but the first would always stick with me.

The car wasn't as bouncy back then, but I remembered her blonde hair bobbing in a long curl at the end of her ponytail. We had the same backpack shoved beneath our legs. Both sets of knobby knees covered in haphazard scabs, old and new. She filled a void my dad had left behind. A fated sister I never knew I wanted until I had her. Until I lost her.

Silent tears streamed down my face as I pulled the clunker against the curb a few stores down from Lupe's shop. If there ever was a need for therapy, it was in that moment.

The bell above the door clanked, alerting my arrival. Lupe's grandson, whose name I still didn't know, leaned onto one metal crutch as he hovered over a *Mini Trucker* magazine laying open on the glass counter. His eyes drifted lazily up to meet mine.

"Hi," I said, smiling brightly and waving like a doof. "Miss me?"

He snarled and grabbed his other crutch. Hobbling around the counter, he met me before I could get to the curtain. "Ey, I don't think so." He held a crutch out to block me, balancing on one foot. "You owe me a gun."

Glancing at his bum leg, I sized up my chances of suddenly becoming Chuck Norris. "Sure thing. Comes with ten rounds. Call that the deposit." I nodded toward the gunshot wound that had left him temporarily crippled. "Look." I raised my hand. "I don't have time to get into shit with you right now, man. I've got some headless dead bitches hot on my tail, and unless you want to get caught in the crossfire, I'd get the fuck out of my way." I hoped upon hope that for once someone else could see my specters and one would come shambling through the front door at just the right moment and scare the shit out of him.

"She's busy."

"She'll want to see me."

"You don't know who's in there."

"You don't know who's in *here*." I tapped my temple and stepped closer, eyes wild, my nose nearly touching his. "Hell, sweetie. And I'm not talking Vermont Square. I mean fire, pitchfork, little cloven hooves, hell. And I survived. So trust me when I say—"

"You're sure?" Cyrus's voice whispered from the other side of the curtain.

"Hell? My ass—" I clamped my hand over Gimpy's mouth. Widening my eyes at him, he got the hint and shut it so I could eavesdrop.

Inaudible whispering brought me closer to the curtain. I held tight to the grandson's mouth, dragging him with me.

"These warnings would have been appreciated beforehand." More whispering, so low it sounded like the hissing of a pipe. "Not if I could stop it." Whispers. "As far as it took." Hissing. "I would have enlisted the help of someone who would." Quiet.

"How long has he been here?" I whispered to the grandson.

"Mum-ph-herf." I moved my hand, and he tried again. "Not long. Ten minutes. Why?" His whisper wasn't as quiet as mine, and soon the shuffle of feet was on us.

"They're talking about me," I said so low I couldn't hardly hear myself.

"Why?"

I pushed away from him and muttered. "Because I brought hell back with me."

The curtain parted quickly, and Cyrus's green eyes locked on to mine. "Not who I expected to see." His brows pulled together.

"I'm having a little trouble." I walked past the grandson. Cyrus moved to let me pass.

"Really?" His light tone oozed with buried dread. "With what?"

"Dead things." I sneered as I passed him. Lupe's eyes were tired, and the youthful glow from the Cyrus mojo had given her seemed to have faded. Though her ragged complexion was gone, her age showed through her eyes. "Tell me why Regina was at my apartment today." I didn't wait for her to greet me. "Or the brunette… what was her name? Oh, that's right, you don't know. No one does because they're fucking dead. *Dead.* And strutting their stuff down Mesa Boulevard. Marienne, dead. Zoran, dead. Azelie, I lopped her head off. Why, oh why, are headless rotting corpses *still* haunting me?"

She chewed on the stubbed end of her cigar. “And of your devil?”

“What?” Her eyes narrowed until I got the hint. “He’s gone.” I shook my head.

“And you can be sure?”

“Look, I shoved a bag of Dad dirt in the dude’s mouth and sent him packing. Haven’t seen him since.” I shrugged. “Not a peep.” Except the lingering desire for sex and bacon. And possibly communing with the dead.

Two brown eyes glared at me. “But you’re haunted by these girls?” I nodded. “Why did you come to *me* with this?”

“Because you’re the badass witch that dropped me into hell. I figured you had a few insights.” I looked back and forth between the two. “What the fuck is happening?”

Cyrus stepped forward, ready to fill me with falsities. “Dylan—”

“It’s like a cold.” Lupe cut him off. “Sleep, eat, you’ll feel better. You were dead. What do you expect?”

I blinked at her a few times. I didn’t really know what to expect on my return from hell, but it sure as fuck wasn’t old shit coming back to haunt me. Shambling corpses seemed so mundane in comparison to wherever the hell I’d been fighting demons like a fucking Winchester and shit.

“I didn’t expect to be standing here again. I thought this was finally over. I thought I’d finally nabbed the bad guy.” I leaned against the square pillar that held up the center of the room. “What more do I have to do to just be normal again?” I used the dreaded N word and for once it felt good.

They were silent. Cyrus folded his arms over his chest and glared at Lupe who refused to look at anyone; instead, she fiddled with the cards she seemed to always have.

"This is difficult to explain, but from what I understand there could have been complications in your transition from the otherworld." Cyrus refused to look at me while he spoke.

I lowered my brows. "What kind of complications?"

"It's not a definite, only a possibility." He held out his hands defensively. "Because Lupe couldn't bring you back right away she—*we*—don't quite know what did eventually pull you back in. The unpleasant… odor you have, according to her highness, can be a sign of a soured soul."

"A what?" Disbelief filled my words.

"Oh, stop the sugarcoating, boy," Lupe snapped at him. "You died. I'm sorry." She talked around her iconic cigar. "You shouldn't be alive, but you are. "Be happy. Get married. Have babies. Live your life."

Cyrus scoffed. "That's your answer? Live your life?" He planted his hands on his hips and shook his head. "You never change, do you?" He looked at her, sorrow in his eyes. "Decades have passed, and you're still only out for yourself. Never accept blame for your shortcomings." Cyrus scolded the old woman like he was her father. For all I knew he was.

"You listen here, boy. Your relationship with Nicolas was the only reason I allowed you in this shop in the first place. My debt has been paid twice over. I owe you nothing and owe her less than that. Before you start spouting off about blame, point that finger at yourself. Magic comes with no guarantees. Heaven and hell are fickle beasts and will not be tamed by the likes of me. Your friend is alive, are you not happy? You finally hold the title you have been waiting for. You are king of all you see. Are you not happy?"

"Happy?" I slapped my thighs with both hands. "You want us to be happy? Your *help* has done nothing. Your help sent me to the otherworld—to hell—after a soul that had long since passed. Your help killed me. I don't know why I'm back but I sure as fuck know it wasn't because of you." I jabbed my finger in her direction. "You have two eyes again, thanks to him, aren't you happy? Your treasonous grandson has been wiped from oblivion because of me, are you not happy?" I stepped closer to her. "You want happy? Tell me why I still have this." I held my tattooed arm toward her. "Tell me why I'm being haunted by dead things sent to me by a woman who's been dead nearly two weeks. Tell me when I can expect what I know is lying in wait and what I can do to kill it. I'm done with you and your help. Tell me what I need to know and you'll never see me again." She scoffed. "Don't help me"—I leaned toward her dramatically—"and I'll bring hell with me to your doorstep."

Her eyes widened a smidge, but she hid it away quickly. "You think you have that power?"

"No. But you do, and that's all I needed to know." I looked at Cyrus. "What is she not telling me? Don't play stupid because I already know you two are hiding something."

He let out a long breath. "I should have never brought you here." *Duh.* "We were desperate, and I knew she could help. Sandorus saved her life when Azelie took her leg, and in fifty years, she never repaid that debt." His timeline put young looking Azelie on the cougar list. "Had I known any of this was down the pike for you, I would have taken care of Azelie myself."

"Ha," Lupe laughed. "What could you have done, pussycat?" Her condescending tone brought me back to the first few times I'd met her. "You need me, and I needed you. So what, I skimmed a little off the top first. I did what you asked and more."

"I shot your living grandson and threatened your life. It

wasn't as though you did it out of the kindness of your heart. What exactly did you skim off?"

"Well, eh." She flipped her hand in the air, poo-pooing the notion. "He had what I needed. What would you have done, eh?"

"She lied to you," Cyrus admitted. "She lied to you to get to me." He glared at the old woman, blatantly accusing her of subversion. "She continues to lie because she's not done with me yet and she knows she can use you against me. She'll bleed me dry with the promise of your salvation." His eyes didn't move from hers.

"Oh, so dramatic." She didn't deny it.

I couldn't believe someone would go as far as damning another human being to hell for personal gain. "You knew?" I hissed. Betrayal seared my core. It wasn't surprising in the least. Why had it ignited the burning pit brewing in my core?

"Beasts of hell are often excellent liars." She explained away her extortion. "I simply didn't bother to question the knowledge I pulled from your head."

"I fought off a beast of hell to save a soul you knew couldn't be saved?" Shrill, my voice echoed uncontrollably through the concrete room. "I died. I fucking died so you could play magical Betty Crocker with Cyrus?" I growled, fire raging, and I stomped toward her. "So what is this? Huh?" I said, flashing my evil ink. "Do you even know? Come on, Ms. All Powerful. Tell me the truth. What the fuck is this?" My words fell over her like lava from my molten center.

"It is a mark put on you so a demon can find you," she said after a long pause. "Something like that takes immense power and vengeance. Santa Maria, I swear, these things are not from me and cannot be summoned in this shop. I do not practice the magic that can summon such a thing." She looked away from me. "I do not have the power to stop the magics put upon you." Her voice shook, nearly trembled with fear. She kept it hidden well, but I'd be damned if she wasn't afraid of me.

"Oh, really? I thought you were some kind of big deal?"

She laughed, throwing her head back. "Yes, but only God can help you now." Her brown eyes met mine and held them for an uncomfortable few seconds. "You are forsaken, *mija*. For you, there is no God."

"So all this believe in yourself, have faith in your own womanly prowess, fight your own demon pep talks were all bullshit? A line of crap so you could score mystical lion blood?" The woman I'd counted on to save my cursed ass was nothing more than a backroom fraud. Welcome to the land of the living where everyone fucks you, but no one leaves a ten on the dresser.

"Not bullshit. Now more than ever your own instinct is the first line of defense against what haunts you. But, you are on your own. I cannot help you any further. I will not." Her fear had been swallowed down, hidden away where I couldn't see it. I knew the dance well.

I let my head drop into my hands, fighting the urge to cry and battling the need to rip her fucking throat out. "What do you suggest I do with myself then? Because at this rate, someone is going to get hurt or I'm going to end up in the nuthouse. Probably both knowing me."

Lupe shrugged apathetically. "Find the source. Stop it."

"Dylan," Cyrus called my attention after being silent so long, "can we agree on who may have done this to you?" His expressive eyes told me he'd been aware for a long while where my demon had come from. My mind was blank for a moment before a familiar face popped into my memory. I nodded, knowing full well who'd sent it to me. His breathing heavy, he set his jaw tight before he whispered. "Are you willing to do what it takes to make this stop?"

"I went to hell and back. I think the answer to that question is a resounding yes." I knew what he meant. Someone, a human someone, might have to die in order to save myself. "It may not have to come to that. Before I died, I was seeing that… thing in my dreams. It haunted me. But now, nothing. Only the girls. And maybe my dad, but I can't be sure that was reality or my own head." It felt good to say those words out loud. Piecing together the puzzle, I turned to useless Lupe and hoped she would answer a few more questions honestly before kicking me out of her shop for good. "Could Azelie's curse, me seeing these dead girls for the rest of my life and living in that guilt, be permanent even after she died?" I hoped the answer to that was yes. While headless dead bitches were shocking, they were nothing compared to the demon that stalked me. I could learn to live with the dead, demons, on the other hand, could fuck off.

Not looking up from her cards, Lupe nodded. "Possible. Curses can live on in a talisman or verve if it isn't destroyed." I recalled the voodoo doll Zoran held the night shit had hit the fan.

"Is there a chance that is all this is? And the hell stench is just a remnant of pulling myself back to life which will go away with time?" I grasped at every straw I could drum up.

"Of course." I let out a tiny sigh of relief. *Of course* could have meant anything, but it was what I needed to hear at the time. "Then again, I could be lying. Eh?" A sinister laugh bubbled up her throat.

"I should have killed you when I had the chance. I'd have

been better off buying my curses a beer and calling a truce." I flipped her off, but she didn't bother looking up at me to see it. She made it clear she was done with the both of us. "Fuck this. I've got a funeral to plan." I turned on my heel and stormed toward the curtain. "Take that wooden leg and shove it firmly up your ass," I said under my breath. Stopping at the doorway, curtain pulled back, I turned to face her. "I'll be sure to tell my demon where to find you when he comes looking for me. Surely a woman of your skill set would come in handy for a beast looking to crawl up from the depths." My threat didn't seem to do much, but deep inside me, my fiery hunger rumbled, and for a moment I felt vindicated.

"Dylan," Cyrus called after me as I made my way to the front door. "I cannot apologize enough for any of this."

I shook my head and pushed through the door. It jingled on the way out. "Did you know?" I asked candidly. "Did you know anything? I need you to be perfectly honest with me now because my dead little heart can't take any more of this and I just might lose control over whatever this is brewing in my belly."

Dude, what is this a Pepto-Bismol commercial?

His mouth gaped. "I know I've not been frank with you, but I'm no sadist. People like Lupe, those with power, tend to be narcissistic by nature. Some don't know any other way to be. I knew when I contacted her your price would be steep, and I was always prepared to help you. Azelie d'Entremonte was a heartless, soulless woman in her life and there was nothing I could have done to stop you from finding her because that is what she wished." He laid an open hand in the center of his chest. "Lupe… *I* brought you to her. I did this to you."

Closing my eyes, I tried desperately not to agree with him on all counts. "Did you know what could happen to me? Did you know Tatum… wasn't real?"

He looked away from me. "I knew Lupe had every potential to use your situation to her advantage. I knew, and I didn't care. For that, I am responsible. You needed her. You needed her because of me. What else could I do? I should have never let this happen. I should have never allowed this." His trembling hands ran through his hair. Vulnerable and emotional, I'd never seen Cyrus so wholly human.

I nodded. "No, you shouldn't have. But what were you going to do to stop me?" In the long run, coincidence and magical intervention aside, I'd really done it all to myself. "If we're being completely transparent here, and this doesn't leave this conversation, I should have left those dead hookers to fizzle away just like Tatum had." I kicked the ground, angry at myself for falling victim in the first place. "Barring time travel, there's no going back now. Tomorrow is the only thing I can strive for. Without the half-assed guidance of Lupe, I'm flying blind here."

We stood in silence for a few seconds. Which was longer than either of us preferred. "What now?" Cyrus asked, shoving his hands into his pockets.

I watched the clouds move across the sky for a moment. "Now, I wing it. I was always better at that anyway," I said quietly. "Thanks for trying. Even though you fucked-up royally." I patted him on the shoulder with a chuckle.

"I'll accept that," he said humbly.

With nothing more than the hope that all I needed was time and patience, I glanced back into Lupe's botanica one last time. "Just do me a favor, okay? Don't let Mike send me to the funny farm." He nodded vigorously. "At least not until I know for sure there's no other explanation for all this." I hadn't discounted the notion that I'd just come back wrong, but I knew how the world worked, and it was never that simple. "Now, enough screwing around. I've got a dead girl to bury. Let's just hope I don't fuck this up."

Cyrus's face softened. "Please let me come with you. I feel somewhat responsible for this… situation."

"You have no idea how many fingers of blame I'm fumbling at the moment. Your involvement in my life and the place I am today is above God and below me, so it looks like you can live guilt free for the time being."

He rolled his eyes unattractively. "Listen, we'll discuss semantics later. Right now, you need help, and I'm your guy."

I blinked a few times, stuck in the realization Cyrus had slowly become a real grown up in the six months I'd known him. His bumbling sidekick routine had rolled away with Malcolm's head, and he seemed the better for it. Although, there was a part of me that wondered if he had just been full of shit all along.

Who is Keyzer Soze?

I wasn't sure why he'd ever want to accompany a crazy girl to plan her dead best friend's funeral, but deep down, I knew it might be a good idea. With him around, Mike wouldn't be so hyper-focused on me, and maybe it could help me hide my dead girls.

"Fine. But isn't there big shit going on at the O.K. Embrace?" House of Porte bigwigs in town may have been worse than my New Orleans detective.

"Yes." He closed his eyes dramatically and used his large hand on my shoulder to guide me toward Mom's car. "Which is why I will be nowhere near it anytime soon."

"I have it on good authority you can't hide from bullshit

forever." So say the headless bitches on my tail.

"Trust me, I'm aware. But I can allow Dominika to take the reins and warm them up before my grand entrance."

"Oh, so this is all a show?"

"Fuck no, I'm terrified." He laughed, and his bright white smile flashed. His f-bombs had gotten more frequent since I'd met him too. "After the death of their Primus, the last thing House of Porte leaders want to see is an outsider. I'm being diplomatic. For now."

"Non-vampy Primus. Must be unprecedented."

The bell dinged above the door as a new patron pushed it open. I wanted to shout out to them it was a trap, stop them from whatever hoax they were about to encounter. However, considering the fact they likely didn't have a magical century-old lion guy as collateral, I figured they'd be okay.

"As was Secondus, but after a few decades, they've come around."

The nameless grandson flipped me off from his spot behind the counter as I passed the skinny strip of window between the front door and the next business. I smiled and blew him a kiss. There was no room in my mind for street punks. I had bigger, deader fish to fry.

"Headless dead girls, shiny black demon things, a trip to hell, plus a full-on body takeover and I still can't wrap my head around whatever the fuck you are and how you fit into this vampy conundrum."

"You're not alone." He smiled again and planted a kiss on the top of my head. A more friend-zone version of the one I'd gotten from Mike. "Would you like to ride with me?" He eyed my hunk of metal judgingly.

"No. My mom would have kittens if I left her car in the ghetto."

"Mmm." He nodded and looked around. "It might recognize its natural habitat and refuse to go back home."

"Hilarious." But true. "If you're killing time, might as well act as dead girl buffer. Don't tell Mike, please. He just doesn't get it." He'd have to get with the occult program eventually if he wanted to try to be a thing again. I had a visceral awareness the occult wasn't going to let me go with a few days rest and some bacon.

"I understand." He'd seen it firsthand.

"Thanks. You know, I hate most people. I don't hate you."

He squinted his eyes and held his mouth tight and disagreeably. "I do believe that's the most sincere thing you've ever said to me."

"Eh, well. Don't get used to it." I punched him on the arm and pulled my keys from my back pocket.

"Wouldn't dare." His eyes glistened a bit and a look passed over them that worried me.

"If I'm dying or some shit, you better tell me," I said suddenly, questioning what I'd seen in him.

He appeared offended, but it could have been an act to cover up more bullshit. "I know nothing more than you do. I came here today for that very reason. Answers."

I looked at my feet while I chewed on the inside of my cheek. I didn't want to believe he'd let me live in danger, but I also didn't put it past him to possibly think of himself first. Power, he had, and narcissism wasn't too far off. "I'm counting on you to be my supernatural sounding board. Just know the last man I counted on with my life wound up dead." It was my father, and I had nothing to do with it, but the idea was there, and that was all that mattered.

"Sure." His cocky smirk made my cheeks flush in an odd mix of lust and anger. "I know for a fact you're a dreadful shot." He ran his hand along his stomach under his shirt. I knew he had to be feeling along the fleshy pink scar left over from my bullet.

"You're a horrible liar." My honest reaction to his obvious subject change didn't catch him off guard.

"And here I am with all these years of practice." His eyes moved slowly away from me and inspected the sky for a moment. Gray clouds had been moving in on us. "You'd better hurry if you plan to make that appointment."

"Yeah, she won't bury herself." I cringed at my shitty joke, and he graciously ignored it.

We parted with an awkward smile. He was lying, I knew it. Azelie was an easy scapegoat, and I'd jumped on it just like I was certain Lupe had intended. There was more to me and my trip to hell than he was willing to tell me. So much more. It couldn't have been that easy. Dying and living were more complicated than that. My life was more complicated than that.

Living dead girl, interrupted.

SIX

“HOW MUCH IS IT?” I ASKED, ASTONISHED AT THE COST OF death.

“Miss, the satin lining is the most luxurious. Your loved one deserves the best in their eternal rest.”

“Eternal rest.” I scoffed under my breath. “She’s going to be cremated. I could shove a secondhand prom dress in there with her, and it’d be all the same in the end.” I’d held in the tears too long, and my sadness took shape in the form of irrational cynicism. I let out a long, calming breath. “Isn’t there an economy version?” The woman closed her eyes and lifted her brows. “I know, you’ve explained, I *have* to purchase a body box of some kind because of state regulations. Got it. What I’m saying here is, thousands of dollars to roll a wooden box into a fire…” I raised my brows back at her, waiting for her to catch the hint. “Is fucking ridiculous,” I spat out, slapping my thighs when she didn’t figure out my sarcasm.

“Ma’am.” I’d gone from miss to ma’am. Apparently, I’d hit a nerve. “I understand there are financial difficulties. Perhaps I can refer you to our sister facility in Mission Junction.”

She looked me up and down, judging my lack of money. I cocked a brow and a hip.

“Your business is with the dead. Unless you plan on not only being an employee, but also a client, I’d suggest you change your tone.” Mission Junction. She had to mention Mission *fucking* Junction.

“Finances are not an issue,” Cyrus piped up from the back of the room. He’d insisted on joining us for the planning, to the chagrin of Mike who had been successfully pouting for a solid hour. “Satin is also not an issue. Tatum Price is dead. Bleeding the family dry is a cold, manipulative thing to do and you should be ashamed of yourself.” He hadn’t been rude, or cruel, but his honesty scratched across her face contorting it into a mess of anger and humiliation.

I eyed Cyrus, hoping to not have the money talk right there. “On behalf of McTavish and the Western Cabal, it is my pleasure to offer whatever monetary compensation you require.” He spoke to both the bitchy lady and me.

Hiding a smile from Mike, I mouthed thank you for only Cyrus to see. Tatum had her affairs in order, more than I ever would have, but in terms of satin and frivolous things, I had no idea where she stood—or laid stiff—on the issue and couldn’t see blowing her money on it. Especially since she’d specifically asked to be cremated. Seemed pointless to burn up a perfectly good, overpriced dead-person box. Cyrus’s money, or really Malcolm *ginger-fuck* McTavish’s money, on the other hand, I was happy to spend.

A sinister grin spread across my face. I turned to glare at the woman behind the desk. "Take your satin lining and shove it right up your—"

"Dylan," Mike hissed, and I stopped. "We'll take the *Economical Traveler*, please."

I scoffed. "Travel where? She's dead," I grumbled and sat back in my chair. "I should have just sent her off to Valhalla myself." Viking style.

Flustered, the woman shuffled papers around in her hands and stacked them nervously against the desk. "Well, I think we're just about done here then. Some paperwork for you to sign, Mrs. Hart."

"*Miss*," I corrected.

"I'm sorry, I thought...." She pointed to Mike, whom she had already worked with during my "vacation," but considered Cyrus in the situation and stopped herself.

A menacing smile cocked one side of my mouth, and I winked at her. That woman would think whatever she wanted about me. If that included a sexual relationship with two dudes, so be it. In fact...

Dirty birdy.

"Have you thought about where she will be housed?" Cyrus asked, referring to Tatum as a person instead of a dollar sign.

I hadn't thought about where I'd put her when all was said and done. In fact, the idea of an urn hadn't even crossed my mind as I considered her final plans, but that had been what she wanted. I didn't really have a house for myself let alone the cremated remains of my dead best friend. "I guess she'll come home with me." Seemed right. Fair enough punishment to have to look at the thing I'd done for the rest of my life. Hell, I'd probably end up just carrying her around town like Anna Nicole Smith with her Howie.

"We do have a beautiful memorial wall where the urn may be kept. It does allow other family and friends the opportunity to visit and pay their respects. There are a multitude of choices for lovely bronze or gold markers to memorialize your loved one for decades without weather." Her sales pitch grated on the last raw nerve I had.

"Listen here, bitch, Tatum Price was the only person I had on my side. She made stupid choices and on regular occasions could be an all-out cunt, but I'll be damned if you and this bullshit operation gets one fucking penny from me or anyone else on my behalf. Stick her in a cardboard box, burn her up, and hand her over. Or I'll do it myself." Mike stood, and Cyrus moved closer to me. Rage bubbled up from deep within me, my fists shook with it. They were there when the flames took Malcolm and Azelie, when only the charred remains of ancient bones were left smoldering in the pit. They also knew that I was quite close to spilling that can of beans all over that shit sucking place.

"Ma'am." The woman closed her eyes slowly, raising her eyebrows in an annoyed, dramatic fashion. She let out a long exacerbated sigh. "Your attitude is not necessary."

I lifted my butt from my seat to get closer to her, placing both hands on her desk. "Oh, believe me, it is." Cyrus laid his hand on my shoulder.

"Ma'am," Cyrus said softly, expressing his diplomacy yet again. "Your offers are appreciated, but unnecessary. Ms. Hart has expressed her need to move through this process quickly and economically. After this moment, you will not attempt to convince her otherwise. You will sit down behind your little desk and pick up your little red pen. Be prepared to finish this up because we are leaving here in fifteen minutes. Understood?"

The bubbling rage began to settle, but the aftereffects sent my head swimming. Cyrus held tightly to my shoulder and pulled my chair under my butt to sit. The woman nodded quietly and shuffled more papers on her desk with trembling hands.

On autopilot, I listened to her short, stern directions and signed on the X when the time came. Mike stood studiously behind me, hands gently on my shoulders. Cyrus sat beside me, leaned forward, examining every dotted I and crossed T.

Fifteen minutes later, almost to the second, Cyrus stood and took me with him. The paperwork was signed and plans were made. Forty-eight hours later I'd be holding a shiny bronze box with the ashes of Tatum Price inside. No frills. Nothing fancy. Just a small ceremony in the tiny chapel on the cemetery grounds, just in case there was a god and he was waiting on those final rites before letting her in the VIP section of the afterlife. It was the least I could do.

"Thank you," I said, so low I almost didn't hear myself.

"Don't mention it again." Cyrus squeezed an arm around my shoulder. "Darling, I'd love to stay and chat, but my fate awaits me."

"Dramatic."

He lowered his brow. "You have no idea."

"No, not really." And I honestly didn't care. The deep down eternally curious part of me cared. But the rational, just back from hell part gave no fucks about vampire politics. Demons and hell things topped the fucks given list.

"I'm going to go visit my dad before I leave," I said to Mike who was swiftly moving toward my car. He loathed any physical contact between Cyrus and me and would usually do anything to stop it. This time he was passive-aggressively telling me it was time to leave.

He stopped quick and turned on his heel. “I’ll come with you.”

I shook my head. “I’m okay. Just need a few minutes.”

His eyes shot to Cyrus and back to me. “I’ll wait here for you.”

Dad’s spot was just around the bend near the back gate. Not knowing any other funeral home, I figured Mike did his best to stay within my comfort zone when choosing Tatum’s services. I was grateful because it gave me a chance to tell the old man thank you for inadvertently saving my life.

“I won’t be long,” I called over my shoulder to Mike, and I waved halfheartedly at Cyrus who was meandering toward his car.

In the reflection of Mike’s shiny windshield, I caught a quick, forced exchange between the two men who thought they were saving me. The silent motions were slight and hard to make out, but the emotions plastered on their faces said it all. Fear. Cyrus spoke low to Mike and Mike nodded in return. Cyrus patted Mike on the shoulder, who rubbed a hand over his tired face. I made up lines in my head for what they were saying. None of them did me any good.

The sky was beginning to turn a sunset shade of pink in the late autumn evening. While I’d only just begun seeing my shambling friends again, experience told me that wouldn’t be the end, and nighttime never brought anything good with it. This wouldn’t be a long visit.

Walking around the side of the administration office, I made my way toward the back of the cemetery. The last time I’d been to visit Dad, Cyrus and I snuck through the side gate in the middle of the night. Nearly midnight in fact. I didn't need anything from him this time. Maybe solace. Solace was most definitely on the list of shit I needed.

Tree leaves rustled, whistling in the autumn wind. The breeze kicked up loosened dead leaves from the ends of gnarly branches. Fall had always been my favorite time of year. Halloween, cooler weather, and more night hours had always appealed to me. With the exception of May of this year, this autumn had been the worst season in my entire life. I began to seriously reconsider my love of fall and thought perhaps Christmas would turn things around for me. Maybe.

I passed the large granite angel that I recalled as a landmark from the front of the cemetery to only a few rows away from Dad's plot. He lay between that and the big arch around the side of the lot. I found it without trouble and plopped down on the grass to join him in his silence.

"Hey, Dad," I whispered, looking around to ensure no one was watching me talk to myself. No one being Mike. "I'm alive." I laughed nervously. "We did it, Dad. We killed the bastard." *Hopefully.*

A salty tear slid down my cheek and onto my lips. I lay down with my head below his headstone. "Okay," I said. "That's a lie," I admitted, as though he were standing there making me feel guilty. "I… I don't really know what I did, but I think I'm feeling that beastly thing in my soul. Festering. Growing stronger by the minute." I sniffed back snot. "I'm scared." My voice quivered. "I'm so scared, Dad and I can't tell anyone what's happening to me." I flashed on an image of me in a straightjacket. "I'm staying with Mom now, and I'm scared for her. I'm scared she'll find out about me and be in danger. I'm scared I brought hell back with me. I wish you were here." I laughed. "You'd love this shit." I watched the November sky turn gray as thick clouds moved across it. "Vampires, ghosts, zombies, it's all real. Mostly. I hear the Wolfman is bullshit, but my friend Cyrus is close enough in my book."

Clouds swirled overhead, threatening to pour rain on me. "Tatum died." Dad had never met her, but I'd lain on that grass more than once talking about her, so in my head, he knew her. Dead or not. "I killed her," I added. "If you see her, tell her hi. Tell her I'm sorry. Tell her…" Tears rolled down my face. "Tell her I love her." I swallowed back my grief. "I thought she was with me, but I was wrong. It wasn't her. I'm alone now." I closed my eyes, and the wind dried the tears that clung to my cheeks. "Mike's been good about it. I couldn't have done any of this without him. I couldn't do a lot of things without him if I'm being honest." Dad knew Mike like he did Tatum, only in my head. "I love him you know. I never really stopped. Before I left for the otherworld, I promised him I'd love him until I died. That was a big promise, but deep down, I know I can keep it. How could I not? Knowing my life, I'll die tomorrow anyway, and he can move on with someone who can actually be who he needs them to be. Normal."

"That's bleak." I squealed and opened my eyes. Mike stood over me.

I let out a long sigh and closed my eyes again. *Busted.* "It's true."

"I hope not. I kind of like having you around."

"It's not like I'm planning it." *Yet.*

"Warn me?" he said as though it was a possibility I'd know in advance.

Suicide was kind of a big deal. I'd probably fuck it up

anyway. "Kind of defeats the purpose."

"At least give me the chance to talk you down."

I looked up at him. "Deal."

He lay down next to me. His warm fingers intertwined mine, and we lay in silence for a few long minutes. I could have stayed there indefinitely. Rain and all.

"I need to go to Tatum's," I said suddenly, with no real reason, outside of maybe going through her important papers.

"Tonight?"

"Might as well." We were quiet for a handful of heartbeats. "Will you go with me?" I didn't want him to see me freak out when dead shit came to play, but I sure as fuck didn't want to be in that house by myself. With no certainty as to what was in store for me, I couldn't risk being caught off guard. If nothing else, I wouldn't die alone.

"As you wish," he quoted superciliously.

"Shut the fuck up." I laughed weakly as I stood and left him lying there. "Bye, Dad, see you soon," I whispered to myself.

Not too soon.

SEVEN

TATUM'S PINK COTTAGE SAT IN SHADOWS AS I PULLED INTO the driveway. Detective Colorado hadn't left the porch light on. He had seemed more like the type to leave things how he'd found them. Like he should've had manners enough to leave it on as it had been last I'd seen it.

I had no legitimate reason to be there at that moment. Not any I could come up with anyway. We decided against a wake or viewing. She wouldn't have wanted anyone to look at her with plaster smeared across the gash in her throat. There would be no need for a burial dress or items of remembrance. There were surely important papers for me to look for in order to finalize everything, but that could've waited until morning, when the shadows wouldn't have been an issue.

The sun had set but the night was young, and I wasn't in

the mood to go home. November was in full swing and the crisp night air held a chill not often felt in southern California. Mom's faded leather seat squeaked at the springs as I scooted to the edge, one foot out, one foot in. Debating silently whether I was truly insane or just wholly fucked in the head. Whatever unseen force had drawn me there wasn't strong enough to convince me to actually get out of the car.

Mike's headlights filled the cabin of Mom's car. Regardless of my recent visitors, I couldn't fathom entering that house alone. I needed Mike there for one reason. I was scared. Scared to be alone. Scared to die. Or worse, scared to live the rest of my life looking over my shoulder for the next boogeyman. Cyrus would have been preferred company after the shambling dead, but his cabal troubles couldn't wait. It wasn't that Mike was necessarily second banana, only that his particular brand of banana wasn't hip to the supernatural. That was a Cyrus banana.

Jesus, you need to get laid.

"You sure you want to do this?" Mike asked as he walked up the drive to the car.

I thought for a moment on the question, one leg still inside the car. "Can't chicken out now." I shrugged and left the sanctuary of Mom's car. The smoky old A/C smell clung to my clothes just as it had as a kid. The heavy door took extra effort to shut, and when it did, the sound echoed in the neighborhood.

When the front door was open, I stuck my hand in and flipped all the switches on the panel to turn lights on before I walked in. Things had clearly been moved. Shuffled around and somewhat put back where they were. That had been days ago. A musty odor you get when a house is closed up for too long lingered in the air.

I opened the crank window in the front and let the front door sit open. A swift breeze billowed through and ruffled a magazine on the coffee table. I flashed on a dream I'd had some months back where I'd sat in that living room while Tatum lay dead and headless on the floor under a stark white sheet. I'd never had premonitions before, but I'd be damned if that dream hadn't come true. Sort of.

In the kitchen, where I'd scrubbed clean a bowl of blood I'd found in the sink, which I could only assume had been for Malcolm, the bag was missing from the garbage can. Those detectives didn't fuck around. A week's worth of garbage had sat in that can, including the spotless plastic deli cup that had been filled with blood, but they wouldn't find anything. The sponge I had chosen not to use was missing too. I let out a relieved sigh that I'd had the forethought to use and promptly flush paper towels instead. Not that I had anything to do with a container of blood in her sink, but there had been enough suspicion surrounding me, I didn't need to add to it.

"Have you made any decisions about this place?"

Mike's voice startled me, and I yipped. "I haven't even thought about it. I'm doing good just standing up and not killing things." And that was the cold hard truth.

He didn't address my crazy. Instead, Mike let it go and moved to the second bedroom, looking for any last-minute paperwork in her office he wasn't able to get on his first trip when he took possession of her body.

Alone, I wandered through Tatum's house, feeling more and more at home each step I took. My sneakers made little noise on the hardwood for the first time ever. Looking at every picture on the wall, I made my way to the bedroom. I moved easily through the darkened space, recalling every inch without the need for light in the back part of the house.

Opening the closet in the master bedroom, the scent of her wafted out. Sweet, expensive perfume clung to her clothing. I closed my eyes and pulled in the scent. Images of her face flashed in my head. Smiling, laughing, crying, bleeding.

I'd been so pissed at her before she....

She was being such a bitch and then I....

I couldn't bring myself to so much as think those words as I breathed her in. I'd been focused on saving her soul, rectifying what I could, I hadn't given myself the chance to truly grieve over the loss of my friend. Having gone from one fire to another for weeks, there had been no time for anything human. Sleeping and eating seemed to have been all the life I could muster in that time, and even that was shoddy. In the moment, locked in the memory of her scent, I allowed misery to take over, to drown out the horrors and fill me to the brim with the resonating encumbrance of mourning.

An emptiness I'd felt since the moment it happened, the hollow place where my monsters hid away in the darkest recesses, roared to life. The churning lava of rage I'd been fighting since my grand return, but this time it wasn't rage. A deep rumbling tumbled within as something dark and deadly took me over.

"She's dead," I said coldly. "I killed her." My words came without thinking. Pathetic grief poured out of me in a long sigh, dripping like spent vomit from my lips. Once the grief was gone, there was room for something new and menacing. Any parts of me that pitied myself for taking the life of a friend were stomped out as inky darkness devoured me from the inside out.

It wasn't acceptance that filled me, but rather apathy. The memory of my friend clung to me as I began to let her go, as I began to grow cold inside. Pain, heartache, they'd hardened me over the years until I no longer cared for the world, but that was nothing compared to the hollow oblivion I felt standing there drawing in her scent.

"You all right?" Mike asked, standing in the doorway.

"Fine," I said, not looking at him. I held a flowered dress, fingering its cotton fibers.

I wasn't fine. I was far from fine. I wasn't sad. I wasn't anything. I was empty. Except… except for that gnawing hollow blackness engulfing my soul.

"Did you want to pack up some stuff, or maybe take a few things back to your mom's?"

I stared at the floral print. Small blue and pink flowers dotted the black background. I imagined those flowers were tiny, gnawing beasts. Each with its own set of slobbery teeth, drooling leaf-like droplets with each snapping snarl.

"No." I shook my head absently. "I don't want any of this… stuff."

Mike made a disapproving sound in the back of his throat, as though he were beginning to question my motives.

I feigned sorrow and moved away from the closet. "I can't."

All of the emotion I'd felt, all of the sadness I'd held inside, was gone in a blink, in that one moment of memory. In her scent, I was gone. *Poof.* I couldn't let on. He couldn't know. I couldn't let him see what I was becoming.

"Do you?" He looked at me strangely until I clarified, "Do you want any of it?" They had been friends through all the years; it wasn't an odd question.

He looked at his feet. "No." He shook his head. "No. I just want you back to being you. Whatever that takes." He meant that. Whatever it took.

I stopped my eyes from rolling and nodded instead. "I know. I know." I couldn't hold in the apathy any longer so turned and left him standing in the doorway before I said something I would regret.

Makeup and other primping tools lay strewn about the small bathroom counter. As though she'd just walked out to go to work and she'd be back later. Many of her things were somewhere in New Orleans. Likely in the dump after being tossed out in the trash when she and Malcolm didn't return to House of Porte that fated night.

I wondered who was heading House of Porte now that the blood queen was nixed. Surely whoever it was had Cyrus jumping through hoops back at Embrace. Or would soon enough. The southern cabal wasn't on the top of my list of worries, but with the crippling sadness and guilt gone, there was room for curiosity again. Where those feelings had gone, I couldn't know. Why it had gone would certainly make itself known at an entirely inopportune time. What I would do with that dark, empty space was the true question.

My eyes moved leisurely to the mirror. Green piercing orbs stared back. Two black dots in the center, like pools of oil, glistened in the vanity lighting. I didn't recognize myself. Pale and drawn, my usual plump pink cheeks looked every second of my three-days-dead.

Tilting my head, I admired my pallor. “Dead looks good on you,” I said quietly.

I locked on to my own eyes, staring into their endless abyss. Black fanned lashes framed large, dreamy eyes. I’d never noticed their animalistic fierceness before. The eyes of a predator. A beast on her prey. A cocky smile crooked the corner of my mouth.

“Where were you hiding?” I whispered to myself. Maybe all it took was a trip to hell to shed that pesky conscience. With every day that passed, another hang-up was lost. Like a cold, Lupe had said. But it wasn’t the stench of death that was fading. It was me.

I ran a thin finger over my bottom lip. Almost the same color as my skin, my lips mimicked my dead face. Easily my fingers found the cold metal case of Tatum’s lipstick on the edge of the sink. A gentle, expert flick of my fingers twisted the dark red stick upward. Tatum’s lip strokes were still visible on the waxy surface. I examined the markings, eyeing over the curved indent worn away from use. Carefully, I swiped the color across my pale lips. The curve in the stick slid perfectly over the curves of my lips, as though it were meant just for me.

Pressing them together first, I puckered my lips in the mirror. The deep red contrasted my skin making me look ghostly white. I pulled it from its band and fluffed my curly hair.

“Sorry, ol’ girl,” I said to Tatum, who surely couldn’t hear me anyway. “You’re dead, but I’m very much alive.” My brow cocked, a sardonic smile spread across my face. “It’s time to get to living or get to dying." I fluffed my hair once more and gave myself a wink. "Showtime."

I strode confidently into the living room. Mike stood in the center staring at his phone. In his hand a file of paperwork. His broad back and tall form was all man. A long-sleeved shirt hid away what I knew was underneath. Warmth I knew I would find against his skin. Untamed passion I knew I could draw out with little more than a look.

"That was quick. Figured you'd want to go through more things while we're here." He ignored my earlier refusal, likely convinced I'd change my mind.

He finally looked up from his phone. His eyes met mine, and his phone hand lowered. I smiled, not caring what that smile might mean for his perception of my sanity. Deep in the core of my hollow darkness, the fiery hunger rolled through. I'd tried to quell that ravenous beast with meat, but it was never satiated because it wasn't food I craved.

"I think it's fair to say that is entirely accurate." My breath came fast, heaving my chest.

I closed the space between us in a few quick strides. Looking up at him under thick black lashes, I innocently lifted the center of my brows. The feral expression I'd had faded away and I met Mike with a look he preferred. Demure. A damsel to his knight.

He dropped his head and spoke quietly. "What's going on with you?" His voice quivered.

I leaned in close, standing on tiptoes. My lips grazed the edges of his. "Does it matter?"

I'd never felt more alive than the moment I realized I was likely still quite dead.

He swallowed hard. "Not today." His warm breath filled my mouth.

Instant heat ignited between us. His mouth pressed to mine, greasy red lipstick smeared across my face and his. Hands and lips moved frantically. His breath pushed against my lips. Large hands wrapped around my back and pushed their way under my shirt.

The hunger inside me rumbled a growl through my teeth. I pushed my chest against him. The need to climb inside him, to take everything he was into myself, clawed at my bones.

Aggressively, I pulled his shirt over his head and tossed it to the floor. I intertwined my fingers in his hair, using it to pull him to me. I forced his mouth to find mine again. Raw prickling tickled its way down my stomach and between my legs.

My teeth found his lip too easily. He winced in pain when I reopened the small cut from the morning and returned the aggression. Frantically, he pulled my shirt over my head and dropped it to the floor behind me. Fluffs of black waves bounced around my face.

Wrapping strong arms around my waist, he lifted my chest to meet his mouth and laid into my breast with gentle teeth. Blood from his lip clung to my pale skin. His human weakness brought my dark hunger to the surface. I planted my feet and shoved him against the wall, knocking pictures from the shelf beside us. His hands gripped my ass and pulled me closer. Mouths pressed together, his tongue moved through my mouth, and I fought the urge to gobble him up.

A flawless flick of my fingers pulled the buttons on his 501's open, one after the other. His dick pushed against the fabric of cotton boxer briefs, framed by his open fly.

Wrapping my hands through his sandy blond hair again, I pulled him toward the couch. Plopping his ass down, he never moved his mouth away from mine. Unbuttoning my own jeans, I straddled his lap. Lowering myself over the top of him, only the denim of our jeans keeping us apart.

He held tight to my hips, pulling at me rhythmically. Blackness, soulless, remnants of hell scurried to the surface, taking control. Wildly, I sank my teeth into his bare shoulder. Initially, he ground himself against me, gripping tight to me, aching to slip it inside. When the tangy copper taste of blood found my tongue, he didn't like it so much anymore.

Blood filled my mouth. I let it slide down my throat. It wasn't a lot. Wouldn't even need stitches. But the pain was too much for the boy and he pushed me away. I clung tightly with my thighs. Pushing myself against him again. Forcing him to choose the pain or lose the pleasure.

Pulling blood from the wound, I sucked at his skin. He bellowed and squeezed my arms. Finally, he overpowered me. Strong arms shoved me away, breaking the seal I had on him. I smiled, blood clung to the edge of my lip. Breathless, my boobs jiggled with each ragged inhalation. Drunk with pleasure and power, I laughed. A throaty thing that held life of its own.

I thrust my boobs against his face, muffling his words before he had a chance to speak them, and plunged my mouth to the bleeding bite again. He bucked, shoving at me again, but I refused to let go, and pushing his face further into my cleavage.

Hands entwined in his hair, I pulled his face away from my chest and pressed my bloody mouth to his. Feral hunger fueled my lust. I was untamed, wild. I wanted nothing more than to devour every last inch of him.

"Enough," he bellowed and stood, knocking me to the floor.

I looked up at him, a mass of beastly human at his feet. Blood drying on my mouth, his dick inches from my face. I wasn't finished with him yet. I yanked him by his open fly toward me.

"You're not finished yet," I panted, tugging at the band of his boxers.

"Actually, I think we are." He pulled his jeans from my hands. "This isn't you."

Rage snuffed out the hunger, and I stood slowly to my feet. "You are *not* walking away from me," I growled.

He picked up his shirt from the floor. "Am I not doing it right?" he asked, referencing my many great escapes.

Wild eyes couldn't penetrate his defenses. "You're not finished here." Hands on my hips, I stood my ground, but my pride refused to chase him down. I could finish the job just the same with or without him. It was the principle. Michael Petersen did not turn me down.

He stopped at the door. "Get home safe, please." He shut the front door behind him. Leaving me alone in the house.

"Fuck!" I snarled and swiped everything off the coffee table.

With Mike gone, my hunger began to settle from a boil to a simmer. Boobs out for the world to see, Tatum's house sex-wrecked, it was hard to deny I'd not been myself. I'd gone too far. I'd given over to the darkness that crept about inside me, and I'd run off the one thing that seemed to curb it and ignite it in the same breath.

Stomping to the bathroom, I pulled tissues from the box and scrubbed off blood and lipstick. Looking at my reflection in the mirror I loathed the two green eyes that stared back. I wanted to scratch off the pale skin. Peel away the layers of Dylan Hart and greet the world as the hideous beast I was.

A black shadow flickered over my face in the reflection. I stepped back, never moving my eyes from the girl in the mirror. As I stared into my own eyes, the girl in the mirror slowly pulled the corners of her mouth to a sardonic grin. The beast was in me. He was there and ready to take over every cell of me until I was no longer. I picked up a heavy bottle of perfume and chucked it at the girl in the glass. It shattered, but the pieces didn't fall. A million and one sets of green eyes looked back at me as I wailed.

Terrified and feeling mostly human again, I ran from the bathroom, my heavy footfalls echoing through the hardwood. As quickly as I could, I retrieved my shirt from the living room floor and slipped it back over my head. I wasn't staying there another second. Darkness in my soul or not, I didn't sign up for scary-ass shit.

I flung open the front door, scurried down a step backward, locked the door and turned to the driveway without looking twice. At the end of the driveway on the street, Mike was parked with his lights off.

My racing heart thudded to a stop. I'd ripped into him with my teeth, ready to swallow him whole, and there he was waiting for me, making sure I was safe. Any other girl would have melted in her Spanx at the thought, while I wondered if he'd forgive me long enough to squeeze in a quickie in the driveway.

I stopped on the walkway and nodded in his direction. He

turned away from me and looked ahead. He'd waited, but only because he'd never live with himself if something horrible happened to me. I slid into Mom's car and cranked over the key; noisy engine roared to life. Mike waited until I backed out and followed me the ten minutes back to my mom's.

I was suddenly exhausted. All I wanted was to get home and lie in bed for a week. Demonic possession really took it out of a girl. It felt like I'd been running a marathon.

A sex-a-thon.

EIGHT

THE HUSTLE AND BUSTLE OF DAILY LIFE AT THE PRECINCT wasn't exactly what it looked like on TV. No one was answering their desk phone and calling everyone over for a powwow. There wasn't an attractive district attorney strutting through the room stopping them from beating someone with a phone book to get information from them.

Law and Order got one thing right, not a one of them had any privacy. Perhaps in smaller towns with fewer detectives, everyone got an office, but in the larger precincts of LA, that wasn't the case. The few offices there had large windows with blinds, but none of them were closed. The men inside stared at computer screens. Likely filing yet another report. Or looking at porn. Whatever.

Most of the desks were empty. It was the middle of the

morning, so surely they were all out finding bad guys or something glazed. I'd visited Mike plenty of times before, mostly to pump him for information, once to pump him for sex, but that was a lifetime ago. I'd never seen the office so dead.

"Can I help you, miss?" a gruff voice called to me while I stood watching Mike work with a man in one of the few offices with open windows.

"Huh?" I turned to see an aging man in a cheap suit. His thick mustache ruffled under his nose. "No. I'm waiting for Detective Petersen." He squinted an eye at me. "Hi, Dylan Hart." I let an innocent smile spread across my face and stuck my hand out to shake.

He took it obligingly and with a tight grip gave me the two-pump release. "Ma'am."

"Miss Hart." A familiar brusque voice made me cringe, and the beast in me stirred to life.

"Hi," I said curtly, gritting my teeth.

"Didn't think we'd see you again." The man, one of Mike's oldest and dearest assholes, hated me almost as much as I hated him.

"Well, here I am." I shrugged. "Is it okay if I just wait here for him?" I pointed toward Mike's desk.

"Is he expecting you?" the asshole asked.

"Usually," I said sarcastically.

"You familiar with this woman?" the mustache asked.

"Quite." He cocked a wooly brow at me. In his defense, I did run out on his bestie. If someone had done that to Tatum, I'd hate them too. But he'd hated me long before that. Since the moment he realized Mike wouldn't be there to bail him out anymore. Bromance is tricky that way.

"Ma'am, you can have a seat here. Petersen shouldn't be long." Mustache pulled a chair to the side of Mike's desk.

I sat, and Asshole sneered. Mustache recognized the tension and gave no fucks. Obviously Petersen was more loved than Asshole, and as such, his disdain meant nothing.

Mike had followed me home, never once looking at me when he'd pulled away as I shut the front door. I'd sacked out almost immediately and lucked out with dreamless sleep. I awoke bright and early with the weight of serious guilt sitting its fat ass on my chest. In the light of day, rested and focused, I realized what I'd done. I didn't know why or how, but I was different somehow. Untamed. Unpredictable. The empty darkness was still there, flaring to life when it saw fit, but my conscience had gained ground and brought guilt along for the ride. I wasn't awake ten minutes before I was pulling jeans over my ass and heading out the door to find Mike.

I'd called him, a few times, but he never answered. There could have been a million reasons why he didn't answer. It didn't matter. And though I hated to say it, I knew a sorry call wouldn't cut it. Hoping for a meet up over bacon and eggs, I was disappointed when he didn't answer or return my call as I drove to the precinct.

As I sat next to his desk, I fidgeted with the toys that lined the perimeter. Most of the office was clearing out as the lingering detectives headed out for the morning leaving me alone to play. When Mustache finally hustled out the double doors, a tingling curiosity took hold of me. A sensation stronger than the primal need to devour. In that moment, anyway. Without another thought, I rifled through the mess of papers on Mike's desk. Checking to see if the coast was clear, I opened the desk drawer and thumbed through until I found a file marked Regina Laurent.

I made sure I was alone before I flipped the file open. Color photos spilled out showcasing the gore. I'd seen her body in the flesh, so to speak, and puked as a result. Though the photos were crystal clear and in full color, my body did not react the same. It didn't react at all. I stared at the photos, taking in every last pixel. The tattoos that trailed her arms didn't make much sense, but one stood out among them. Azelie's symbol.

Checking the drawer again, I pulled out four more files, each with photos that mimicked Reggie's. Hands bound with hair, heads no longer where they should be.

"What do you think you're doing?"

"Where do you suppose are the heads?" I asked Mike, who stood over my shoulder.

Snatching the files from my hands, he stacked them vigorously, refusing to meet my eyes. "What are you doing here?"

"Answer my question."

"Answer mine first." He flared his nostrils and mashed his teeth together as he took a seat in his chair.

"I was looking at Regina's file," I answered honestly. His eyes closed slowly. I'd hurt him in more ways than one, and while I couldn't repair the damage I'd caused to Tatum, I still had a shot with Mike. "But that's not why I'm here." He rocked back in his squeaky old chair and tilted his head to rest on the top edge. "Look, I—"

"I don't want to talk about it."

"But, there's—"

"No." He shook his head.

"I'm sorry," I said finally.

He closed his eyes, sighed, and leaned forward onto his elbows. Holding his forehead, he cleared his throat. "We don't know."

"Don't know what?"

"Where their heads are."

"Oh. That's something."

"That's nothing. Literally, it's nothing."

"Not true. If someone is taking the heads, they're doing something with them, right? Why else go through the trouble? It's not like we couldn't identify the bodies or anything." He shrugged. "I think the better question to ask is why. What purpose do the heads serve?"

"I'm listening."

I didn't really have a theory, but he'd opened the door, so I rolled with it. "Okay." I thought for a moment. "Before I went to… *Tahoe*, Dominika told me vamps can have babies, but it takes a lot of energy. I think Marienne's motive wasn't out of vanity, but medical necessity. Hiring Azelie was just good business practice." I made the villains out to be misunderstood and desperate instead of the ruthless killers they were. Perhaps the monster I'd become was sympathizing with their plight.

"Yeah, so? Those cases are cold now, and frankly no one cares. They stopped so the media stopped. What does this have to do with Regina?"

I had no idea. "I'm getting to that." Talking out the facts of the case helped me wrap my head around the possibilities. It was usually where Tatum shined. "What if… what if the heads have a meaning just like the blood? Marienne needed the blood to have a baby, probably, so what's to say the heads don't hold some sort of power?" I stood and dramatically paced around him. "What if whoever is killing these girls needs the heads?" Nip the head and heart, or you'll have one pissed-off vampire, I recalled Cyrus telling me before I beheaded two poser vampire boys. "What if their own people are killing them?"

"Go on." He leaned back in his chair, the aging springs squeaked in protest.

"Azelie told me binding the hands, binds the soul. Removing the head ensures the body is dead, but binding the hands makes sure they can't come back. If these girls were working for Azelie and Marienne, recruiting lackeys to do their dirty work, what's to say the local cabals aren't taking justice into their own hands? We've gone under the assumption these girls were all… *human*," I whispered. "What if the heads are gone because that is the only means of death? All of these girls bit it around the same time, right?"

"Regina was the first. The others continued over the last five months."

"Hmm. Maybe look into the exact dates. There could be something there. I'll ask Cyrus. Maybe he can help fill in the vampy gaps."

"Please don't." He held up his hand and closed his eyes.

"Why?" I stopped pacing.

He shook his head. "Do I really have to explain?" I waited. "Because I'd rather you separated yourself from those people. For your own wellbeing. Please." He rubbed his sore shoulder unconsciously.

"*They* didn't do this." I placed an open hand on my chest. "Azelie did this. I think."

"Did what exactly?" He folded strong arms over his wide chest.

"Ruined me." She'd started the ball rolling anyway.

He shook his head again, sighed, and pulled me by the hand to sit in his lap. "You'll get better. Trust me. Just stay away." In his mind, it was all in my head and I'd get over it. Little did he know I wanted nothing more than to gobble him up.

"You can't say that for certain." I figured Lupe would've been the best bet to getting to the bottom of my growing darkness, but without her, I would be lucky to survive.

"Nothing is certain. But I'm not going to let it, whatever this is, consume you. If that means guilting you into stepping away from that scene, then so be it." He tucked a stray hair behind my ear. He may not have said it out loud, but he'd forgiven me the second he'd stormed out of Tatum's house.

"These girls deserve justice. Their killer deserves whatever he has coming to him."

"You deserve to know the truth?" His eyes met mine.

"That too." He hit the nail on the head. There was a part of me that cared once upon a time, but that *me* had been swallowed by darkness. Morbid curiosity and the need to survive fueled me now.

He bit the inside of his cheek. “Look, I’ll come by and get you later. We can go pick up your car. Snag some food?” His eyes refused to fix on one spot, especially on me.

“I can handle that.”

When he wouldn’t meet my eyes, I gripped his chin and forced it. Whatever was consuming me didn’t know who it was up against. And like Lupe said, Michael Petersen was my tether. Bound to the earth by one thing. I’d been stupid plenty of times in my past, and if I could get away with it, I’d never tell him what really churned deep inside me, but I sure as fuck knew better than to walk away from him again. He’d be mine until the darkness finally took me. Every. Last. Inch.

“Petersen,” Asshole called from across the room. “Say it ain’t so?” he begged, strutting toward us. “I thought we talked about this?”

Suspicion reared its vengeful head. “You talk about me at work?”

“Not exactly,” he said under his breath. “Linkerman, don’t be a dick.” Mike’s response didn’t instill fear in the heart of Charles “Chuckles” Linkerman. Asshole extraordinaire and supreme screwer of my life. I’d nearly forgotten about the poor ginger bastard in the time I’d been out of the picture. He was still an asshole. And I’d be damned still a goddamned ginger.

“Who’s being a dick? All I’m saying is, we talked about this.” He flicked his finger back and forth between Mike and me. “Months ago. I thought this was a done thing? What about Maria?”

“Who the fuck is Maria?” I asked, suddenly unreasonably jealous of some unknown girl.

"My sister."

"A Linkerman?" I laughed and looked at Mike. "Oh, that's rich."

"Nothing happened," he said quickly and went back to his boy in blue. "Your sister's a sweet girl, but she's not really my type."

"No? I thought you liked them heavy?" he asked, looking me up and down.

My body tensed with instant rage. I'd been called a fatty by the best of them, but hearing it from Chuckles in front of Mike was too much for my broken psyche to take. I stood and raised a fist unconsciously. Mike reacted swiftly and retained me before I let it fly.

"Whoa, control your broad, man. Not too smart hitting a police officer in the police department, eh?" His weaselly laugh matched his weaselly face. Watching his freckled cheeks turn his hazel eyes into half-moons reminded me of Malcolm McTavish, and I realized suddenly why I'd hated him instantly. Sucked for him.

"Now is not the time," Mike whispered. "Kick rocks, Chuck." Mike shot him a glare, bringing Linkerman's hands up in surrender.

"Fine. Fine. But don't hate me when I say I told you so. Because you know as well as I do, I'm going to say it eventually."

As he walked away, I turned my head slowly toward Mike. "I understand I have no right to ask this but in the name of monogamy, who the fuck is Maria?"

"Linkerman's sister. Trust me when I say there isn't a

catastrophic event large enough to force me into that woman's bed. Ever." He shuddered. "*Ever.*"

Jealousy aside, his reaction lent pity for the girl. More than once in my life someone had reacted to me in a similar manner. A small part of me wanted to force him to take her out on a date on principle.

"I'm not trying to play jealous girlfriend or anything, just need to know if I'm going to have to cut a bitch." I patted the top of his head and walked around the desk. "Since you're not pissed at me, I can go about my day of doing nothing." And steering clear of dead things and voodoo priestesses.

"Jealous girlfriend works for me." His honesty was refreshing and creepy. "I know this probably isn't permanent, but whatever this is,"—he waved his hand over me—"it's good."

This—I mentally waved a hand over my body—*is the hollow center of a soulless dead girl.* "Thanks. I'm trying," I said and cocked a smile. He'd forgiven my love bite, but if I lost control again, there was no telling what I could do to rectify my actions.

"Stay out of trouble, kid." He shot me a wink.

"Yeah, right." I scoffed and sauntered out the double doors.

Flip-flopping between good cop and bad cop was playing hell on my nerves. As time passed and the hollow pit settled in, it became apparent I was going to need to formulate a plan B. Spending a full day with the hope a good night's rest and a romp in the sack was all I needed, an incendiary plan of attack was never made. I would be forced to go to the source of the curse I thought I'd exterminated. I found it hard to believe tiny tweaker Angie could unleash a hell beast capable of tricking a human soul into hell only to ride that human right out into the harsh light of day and wreak havoc on the world. Or star in a badass metal video. Trippy.

This is your brain on Satan. Any questions?

NINE

SHE WASN'T OLD BY ANY MEANS. FIFTY WASN'T SQUAT IN the grand scheme of things, but she sure as fuck was time stuck. Mom's computer. Circa 2005, that top of the line desktop featured Windows XP and Internet Explorer. Perfect for those hours you wanted to kill surfing a few web pages.

Two empty beer bottles teetered on the top of the roll-top desk. Frustrated grunts and rapid mouse clicks filled my lonely silence. I would have been better off just going to the library. Only what I was looking for, I didn't want anyone else to see.

I started with the phone number. It was the best bit of information I had to go on. The address she had given me when I'd called her was written on the back of the paper I'd found after a frantic search through every pair of jeans I owned. Having not been around for a few weeks to do any washing helped immensely. Should the need have arisen, I knew Fresno wasn't too far for vengeance.

Junkies weren't known for brilliance, so I assumed just calling her up on the phone was a good first step. Calling from the house phone, I used the special code thing to block my number. It rang, incessantly, before a generic voicemail picked up.

"I'm calling for Angela. I have information on the disappearance of your friend." I paused, not sure if what I had planned to say next was the best idea. "If you ever want to know where he is, you will meet me Friday at nine in the morning." I wanted to ensure I had Tatum good and buried, or burned, before I moved on to saving my own ass. Two days was plenty of time to get my shit together. I left the address to Sween, knowing full well Cyrus would not only allow it, but assist should I need him.

The phone beeped when I pushed the end call button. There was no certainty she'd even get the message. I'd be there regardless. Waiting. Ready for a fight. I'd gone to hell and back to save Tatum's soul. It was my turn for saving.

Surfing the net for answers was useless. The phone number went to a disposable cell therefore untraceable and majorly useless unless she got my voicemail and decided to meet me. The address I had connected me to the name of the apartment complex and the number for a management company. Mike would have been an asset in the hunt, but he didn't know about my trip to Fresno, and I wanted to keep it that way.

"Hello," a gruff voice curtly answered the phone.

"Hi, my name is Tatum Price, and I'm calling with regard to a tenant of yours." I lied through my teeth.

“I can’t give you any information.”

“You don’t even know who I am or why I’m calling.” I responded as politely as I could.

The man scoffed. “I don’t care who you are. My tenants don’t pay me enough to be their answering service. Someone owe you money? Find them yourself.”

I fumed. Frustrated, I said the first thing that came to mind before he hung up on me. “This is *Detective* Tatum Price with the Los Angeles homicide department, sir. One of your tenants was the last person to see a man missing from your area. You ready to help me now?” Impersonating an officer was a felony. I realized that and did it anyway. In court, they called that intent. He was quiet but still on the line. “All I need is an alternate address, emergency contact, any other way of contacting her you may have on file.”

“Humph. What’s the last name?” *Fuck.*

“Sir, if I had that, I’d give it to you. I have a name and address. Can you help me?”

“Nope.” *Click.*

I looked at the phone as though it was the offender. “Well, fuck you, too.”

Turning off the computer, I sat back in the cushy office chair, resting my head back. “That was a bust,” I said to myself, my own voice sounding foreign and alarming.

In the silence, the hollow darkness in my core was hard to ignore. I hoped it was nothing more than psychosis manifested from multiple cases of PTSD. Without Lupe’s half-assed help, there was little chance I’d make it out alive otherwise.

Steam billowed from the hot shower. My hair still hadn't gotten a good washing, and with nothing but time on my hands, it seemed like a perfect opportunity to actually follow the directions, rinse and repeat. Scrubbing the dead from my scalp seemed to ease the tension I'd been toting around since I'd been back. It was a wonder what clean hair could do for your mental health.

I towel dried my hair as best I could before slathering it with a product guaranteed to cost a fortune and leave your unruly hair soft and manageable. Not lucky enough to score actual tendrils, my hair generally took on more of a street person look than curly. Happy to see my own stupid reflection in the mirror, I smiled at myself. Feeling more human than hollow, I took the opportunity to make fun of myself. One of my favorite pastimes. Swinging my thick, wavy locks around, I made kissy faces and winked into the mirror.

I'm a Breck girl.

"You're a jackass," I said to my own, mostly normal, reflection.

A shot with the blow dryer to seal the deal and up it went into a ponytail. It wasn't yet five but seeing no need for real clothes for the time being, I slid into comfortable pants and an oversized T-shirt, not bothering with mundane things like undergarments. Mike would likely want to go out for a bite—*er food*—and I would have to put on something more appropriate for public appearances, but until then there was no reason for binding.

The front door opened and closed loudly. The sound of rustling paper bags called to me like a geek to a gold bikini. Food. I padded down the hall with bare feet. My floppy PJ pants covered everything but the tips of my painted toes. Expecting to see my mother in the kitchen, I instantly hugged my body to cover sagging boobs.

"You brought food," I exclaimed.

Mike smiled without looking away from the containers of Mr. Wong's he pulled from the bags. The spicy ginger scent of my general's chicken I knew had to be in that bag somewhere pulled a roar of hunger from my stomach. Nervousness fluttered up my legs at the sensation of hunger. I'd spent the entire afternoon watching TV and lying on the bed with not so much as a negative thought. In fact, there wasn't much thinking involved at all. In the presence of the one person I had to hide it from the most, I prayed it wasn't the darkness coming to life again. When my hollow space didn't ignite irrepressible desire, it was safe to assume I was just regular old human hunger.

"Not that I'm ungrateful for the sustenance, but why didn't you call first? I'd have put on a bra." And underwear.

"And yet you still ask why?" His smile crinkled the edges of his eyes. A few years older than me, his thirty-something was beginning to show. Fortunately for him, it was an improvement. "Taking a cue from your recent meat addiction, I figured showing up with food was a good idea. Besides, I'm in no mood for the public. And if we're being brutally honest here, the public is no place for you unless absolutely necessary." He pulled two forks from the drawer. "Never know when something violent and unexplainable will happen and there I'll be trying to wipe up the pieces before anyone catches wind." He pointed a fork at me. "You feel me?" His smile had faded and he raised a brow at me.

Nodding, I knew exactly what he was saying and secretly thanked the maker he finally got it. "Agreed." Maybe I didn't have to hide from him after all.

"Good. Now, do your best to curb whatever Hell beast is after you now. I'd really like to have at least one quiet, lazy night. No monsters. No dead things. No blood and bullets. Just you, me, and Mr. Wong." He sat at the table, fork in hand. "Not hungry?"

I sat too and stole my fork from his grip. "And yet you still ask." I smiled and stabbed a piece of sweet and sour pork, shoving it into my mouth.

Mike's T-shirt and jeans ensemble told me he'd gone home before picking up takeout. The evening was still young, and he very well should have been tracking bad guys or something. Tax dollars didn't spend themselves.

"I gotta ask," I said, noshing chicken in my cheek, "why aren't you working?"

Raising his brows, his jaw flexed as he mashed his food down to speak. "Funny you should ask." His eyes met mine, and I knew instantly I was in trouble. "I got a call today from my buddy up in Fresno." *Fuck. Fuck. Fuck.* "Thought I should know there was a woman pretending to be a detective using the name Tatum Price." My heart pounded in my chest. Word traveled fast. "I thought, this has to be a coincidence. Because the only Tatum Price in the Los Angeles area I know is dead." His eyes widened. "Why would she be calling an apartment manager in Fresno trying to get information about a tenant?" Shaking his head, he shoved a piece of chicken in his mouth.

"That was fast. Too bad you guys can't work a case that

actually mattered that efficiently." I tapped my fork nervously against my plate. The hollow inside me rumbled, and I felt the urge to unleash. Wanting to spout off in retaliation, I repressed the flittering darkness with a piece of spicy chicken. "Sorry," I said, around food shoved in my cheek. I couldn't give him more than that for fear something more detrimental would sneak out with it. Feeding the darkness seemed to be the only thing keeping it at bay. Mike had been right, I didn't stand a chance out in the wilds of Los Angeles. There might've been casualties.

"I really hoped it wasn't you." He tossed his napkin on his plate and went to the fridge for a beer. "Why?" He popped the cap. Beer guzzled from the bottle neck as he chugged it down. I opened my mouth to offer an explanation peppered with the truth, but he held his hand up. "You know what. No. I don't want to know. As far as I'm concerned, it didn't happen. Just tell me you had a life or death reason. Please." His eyes screamed *lie to me*.

"My entire existence is life or death."

Eventually, he would have to know. The darkness inside wasn't going away like Lupe had said. The only things that seemed to keep it at bay were food and sex, and laziness. Throw in pride, greed, and envy, and I was the whole package. Wrath had been in me since birth, so there was no contest there. Could I really feed it my sins until the day I died? I could learn it's tell and do my best to keep it at bay for a while. A while wasn't going to cut it. I just hoped I could keep Mike out of it long enough to make it stop and he'd never be the wiser. Sure, he'd begun to come around and even joked about my not being ready for the world, but that didn't mean he'd welcome me and my beasty with open arms.

I now pronounce you Mr. and Mrs. Fucked-for-all-eternity Petersen.

"Fair enough."

I silently cursed the arrogant bastard manager who surely called the local PD and ratted me out. Finding Angie would be my only salvation should my dark stowaway not make an unexpected exit. Asking for Mike's professional help would move that project along nicely, but it would never happen. Not only could I not explain how I came about my demon ink, there was no way he could ever learn why. Mike could never know what I'd done for Lupe. For his own sake that was one thing I couldn't tell him. There was no self-defense. No logical, defendable reason for kidnapping. When committing a felony, the fewer people to know about it the better. Obviously.

"Also," I started, looking only at the prongs of my fork, "sorry about that." Pointing to his shoulder with the end of my fork, I refused to meet his eyes.

Subconsciously, he held the shoulder in question. "Only a flesh wound," he joked, but his smile didn't reach his eyes. I scared him. Through all of his joking and worry, he was scared of me. Of what I was certainly becoming. I didn't blame him. I scared myself. Luckily, the new hollow within me had no fucks to give on the subject. As I tried to fight away my feelings of apathy, I questioned why I would even bother. Not caring was better. Hollow was better.

"Still, shit got weird, and I'm sorry."

Now take your pants off.

Mike left the table without another word. Clearing the table, he moved freely through Mom's kitchen. I wondered how often in the last year he'd been there behind my back, eating and drinking with Mom while I was off living a life without them.

Mr. Wong's clung to my ribs like good food would do. Belly full and impossible to suck in, I thanked baggy T-shirts and pajama pants.

"If I say Netflix and chill, is your dick going to come out?" I asked, trying to lighten the mood as he washed up our forks.

He chuckled but didn't bother looking at me as he spoke. "Your chances are significant. But, lying down and doing nothing while mindlessly binge-watching *Murder, She Wrote* is good enough under the circumstances."

"Be still my heart." Years later and he still knew exactly what to say to turn me on.

The communal gray sweats weren't clean, but he put them on anyway. Anything to get out of binding jeans after beefcaking it on Mr. Wong's. I knew the feeling well and didn't talk shit on his fashion choice.

Shoving his hands nervously in the pockets of his sweats, he stood awkwardly beside the bed. "I'm not bringing this up to be a dick, but I need to know where I stand here."

I pulled the covers back, making up the bed for lounging. "Right now, you're standing beside the bed," I said sarcastically.

His face fell. "You know what I mean." Sorrow pulled tired bags out under his eyes.

Actually, I kind of didn't. "If you're asking me if I'm planning on eating you alive while you sleep peacefully beside me, the answer is no. I have no plans to eat you." I made no guarantees it *wouldn't* happen. I just had no intention of doing so.

He sucked his teeth and nudged the edge of the bed with his knee. "No. That's not what I'm asking you." Surprised he wasn't concerned about my mental stability, I dropped my brow waiting on his explanation. He let out an exacerbated sigh. "Am I getting in this bed for the last time or the first?"

A valid question under any circumstances, but in our situation, it was about damn time to shit or get off the pot. Though technically, it wasn't the first. "I hate to make promises I can't keep." The honesty thing usually didn't work out for me, but then again, neither did lying my ass off. I was fucked regardless.

"Okay." He nodded slowly and pinched his lips between his teeth.

Hurting Mike had never been something that made me feel good. It was never about hurting him; beasty or no beasty. I crawled on my knees across the bed. Meeting his eyes, I forced myself to live a moment in his shoes. I'd been a hellacious cuntbag for nearly no reason and yet he still stood there waiting for me to come around. I'd always been flawed and irreparably shattered, but yet he waited. He waited while I ran for my life. I was dead with no certainty I'd ever wake up, and he waited. If nothing else, he deserved to know why I couldn't promise him my life.

"I could be dead tomorrow." He scoffed and rolled his head away. "I could be dead *now*." His eyes came back to me. "I can't promise you my future because I don't know that I have one. I know… I know what you've done for me. What you've given up for me. I don't deserve any of it." He opened his mouth to talk, but I stopped him with a hand over his mouth. "No. Whatever you have to say doesn't matter. Whether you agree or disagree with that, I don't care. I'm an awful human being. I've lived in a dark space most of my life, and that darkness has found a friend in the occult. No matter where I run, no matter who I have backing me up, I've let that darkness in and it's festering inside me." My hand still covering his mouth, only his eyes told me how my confession affected him. "I can't promise myself to you because deep down, I want you as far away from this as possible. Claiming you as mine would be the most selfish thing I've done to date." I moved my hand away from his mouth. "I'm sorry I did this to you." I nodded toward his shoulder but meant so much more than that.

His aqua blue eyes searched mine for what felt like an eternity. I waited, holding my breath for whatever he was keeping secret in those blue eyes. What I'd told my dad had been true. I loved Michael Petersen to the ends of the earth. How could I not?

"Will you just shut the fuck up and kiss me?"

I let out the harsh breath I was holding, and a nervous laugh burst out with it. There had been a part of me that wanted him to agree, put on his pants, and walk out the door never to be seen again. That part was tiny and wimpy and lost to the part of me that wanted nothing more than to devour that man whole. In every way possible.

Wrapping my arms around his neck, I pulled myself up to kiss him like he'd asked. Heart fluttering, memories of our first kiss came rushing back. Nervous fumbling and laughter got us through that night to see many more like it. Only, less nervous fumbling. Laughter had always been there, however.

His strong arms lifted me off my knees, and I fell back onto the bed with a bounce. Mike fell on top of me and covered my lips and cheeks with tiny kisses. The moment had Hallmark written all over it.

I had been hoping for Penthouse forum.

"Can I trust you?" I asked between smooches.

His forehead creased. "Seriously?"

I pushed at him to back up a bit so I could talk without breathing into his face. "Can I trust myself with you? Even when I'm not really… myself?" I needed to cover all bases before plunging in head first. I'd done that once before, and all it got me was a one-way ticket to hell.

He moved his body to lie next to me. "You have a baseline. You know?" He held his hand level as a demonstration. "You're here, most of the time. I know this you. This is the cynical, brilliant, headstrong girl who wouldn't give me the time of day the first time I met her. This you is perfect." Moving his hand down, he explained further. "This you, the soulful, humble, composed woman I've seen on occasion, is here. This you balances out the baseline." He raised his hand beyond the original point. "Here…" He let out a breath. "Here is where you scare me." Clenching his fist, he lowered his hand to lay on his chest. "But I don't run away from shit that scares me."

I scoffed. "No, usually you point a gun at it."

"You and me both, sister." He wrapped his arm around my head and pulled me into the crook of his arm to lie on his chest.

"Cyrus asked me if I'd be willing to die to save you." My heart stopped. I knew the answer. I always had. Hearing him say it out loud made it all too real. "I told him of course I would. But I think the real question of loyalty is if I'd have the guts to kill you to save you from yourself."

My heart thudded to the depths of my body with a comical clank. His heart beat quickly in his chest. The sound of blood soaring through his veins made my stomach rumble.

"Could you?" I wanted the truth. If his answer was yes, I knew he would be strong enough to see me through to the end. Whatever end that might've been.

His heart beat against my ear a hundred times before he answered me. "Yes." His one word relieved an eternity of dread from my body.

Nodding, I couldn't bring words to my lips. It was all he needed to say. I wasn't ready to share my dark secret, but I knew when the time came, he could handle it. He'd do whatever it took to make certain my life on this earth, no matter how short, was worth living. That was all anyone could ask of another human being.

Mike flipped on the TV without pushing for anything more. I was doing well not crying or screaming or fucking or feeding or whatever the fuck my confused body and mind was begging for. JB Fletcher would've had my mystery solved long before Lupe and Azelie got their claws into me.

WWJBD? What Would JB Do?

We'd been in Cabot Cove for no more than five minutes when my eyes fluttered shut. The darkness inside was quiet and still and, for the first time in a long time, I felt normal.

If we'd been lying in bed at Mike's house, I would have thought the last year of my life had all been a dream when I woke beside him. My favorite asshole bird chirped outside the window. A blinding sliver of sunlight pierced the space between the curtains. I closed my eyes hard against it and pulled the sheet over my head.

Mike's bare chest rose and fell with each steady breath. He'd pulled off his shirt at some point in the night without waking me up, which had taken skill. A small patch of thin, dark blond hair sprinkled across the center of his chest. Light penetrated the sheet under which I laid, illuminating his peachy skin. Blaring red scabs surrounded by purple and black speckled bruising screamed at me from his shoulder. Perfect curved imprints showed where my teeth had sunk in. The broken skin, now scabbed over, had nearly encompassed the front of my mouth. If a forensic expert were looking him over, he'd peg me as the bloodsucking culprit in a heartbeat.

Running my fingers over the wound, I winced when the raised brail of my teeth retold the story of the night I'd torn into his flesh. In the bright shiny light of day, I couldn't fathom doing such a thing. But I had. Knowing Mike would be there. Knowing he understood, or was willing to try, made all the difference in the world. I still felt the hollow space inside, but I'd gotten through the better part of twenty-four hours without vamping out. Perhaps my otherworld jet lag was on the mend after all. Maybe all I needed was someone willing to kill me in the name of love. If only he'd been so willing before I sliced along Tatum's throat, I wouldn't be waking up on the morning of her funeral wondering how long it would be before I fucked up and Mike made good on his promise.

Meatloaf was full of shit, man. Anything for love?
Yeah, that too.

TEN

WE WEREN'T PRESENT FOR THE ACTUAL BURNING OF THE body, thankfully that's not how it worked. I'd been doing well enough pretending I was talking about some Jane Doe rather than the lifelong best friend I'd murdered. The budget body box that had an actual name I didn't bother retaining served its purpose cost-effectively, leaving more than enough for a dramatically macabre and over-the-top stone memorial to be erected near Dad's plot, which was really all that mattered. She wouldn't be there of course. I'd decided to bring her home to live with me. Well, die with me. However that worked out.

My hands glazed with sweat under the surprisingly heavy wooden box I gripped for dear life. The box wasn't mine to keep. The funeral director insisted their loner box would be more attractive than the black plastic version hidden within its wooden walls until her urn arrived from the engraver. I didn't have it in me to argue with her. Even my sinful passenger had been quiet on the subject. It didn't matter much to me either way. The only eyes on the thing were mine anyway.

Mike sat beside me, Mom on the other side. Cyrus, Dominika, and a few other vampire lackeys I didn't recognize took up the back row of the tiny chapel. Two guys with press badges sat casually to the side, away from the family and friends. I wasn't sure who they were as Tatum didn't do work friends. I hoped for their sakes they weren't there to cover the murder of the local tabloid journalist offed by satanic cults while vacationing in New Orleans, because that could just get weird. You know, with witnesses around to see me killing them an all.

I'd kept the service quiet, private, and unassuming for just that reason. During my vacation to hell, I'd missed the quick fizzle of her story a few days after her death. Anyone who followed the media in any facet could agree that was how it worked.

The man behind the pulpit rambled on about God and church, and I shot him an annoyed glare. I had been quite specific with my request. A few words, a quick blessing to cover our bases, and that would be it. No one was interested in joining his church nor would any of us willingly open our wallets for the Lord.

The vampires in the group sat stoic, watching the proceedings with little effect. Dominika yawned loudly, and Mom shot her a look over her shoulder. If she'd been within pinching distance, she'd have gotten a turtle snap to the thigh for being rude.

The minister finished up his unwanted sermon with a prayer. Mom and Mike lowered their heads as did the press guys. I didn't bother looking over my shoulder at the motley crew in the back. Obviously none of them were going to burst into flames anytime soon, so there was nothing fun to see back there.

Hollywood, you are a fucking liar and a cheat.

I closed my eyes tightly and repeated the words the pastor said. Not religious by any means, I wasn't much of a prayer unless my ass was in a jam, but judging by my recent visitors, it seemed the time to pray was upon us.

The boisterous man finished with an *amen.* I followed suit and a searing pain burned through my core. Indigestion from the bowels of hell, bile gurgled up my throat. I belched under my breath, the rumble in my chest audible to those closest to me.

Not now.

"What was that?" Mike whispered.

Shaking my head, I refused to believe what I already knew to be true. "I don't know. Nausea I think." Swallowing back the taste of rotten eggs, my heart thrummed quickly in my chest.

Mom's eyes watched me silently as the man thanked everyone and introduced me to say a few words. I was in no condition to do such a thing and shook my head without thinking. Heart spinning out of control, white spots glittered in my vision. Passing out was most definitely an option in that moment.

Pain from an unknown source crippled my thoughts leaving me motionless and unable to snap out of it. Closing my eyes against the pain, I thought again of the words the preacher had said. I thought and thought until I was almost whispering them through pursed lips. Muscles contracted in places I didn't even know I had. As I prayed silently, the pain grew more and more intense. Vomit crept up the back of my throat, threatening to spill over the edge and spew from my lips.

Mike wrapped his arm around my waist. "Tell me you're

okay?" His lips brushed my ear as he spoke in a murmur.

I couldn't. I'd hoped he would be able to tell *me* those words. Out of desperation, I switched gears and thought of Mike. I focused on the increasing crinkles at the edges of his eyes. The aqua-blue eyes they surrounded. Perfect lips and a jawline you could open a beer on. Leaving God behind, I pulled up the memory of Mike and me at Tatum's house. Focusing on the passion between us, I forced my head to live in that moment. Reliving my sins. Quelling the beast I now knew without question squatted inside me like a toad.

Mike's warm hand caressed my lower back, kneading into the flesh. His touch sent a shock wave down to my toes and the vulgar bile I'd been fighting settled and disappeared. For me, the moment lasted an eternity, for everyone else it was a thirty-second long moment of Dylan Hart freaking the fuck out. Nothing new for my nearest and dearest.

"Fine," I fibbed. "I haven't eaten." I lied, and he knew it. He'd watched me pound back two bowls of Cap'n Crunch before we left the house.

"You're full of shit," he said hushed against my ear. His breath tickled the small hairs on my neck and brought goosebumps to my skin.

Patting his other arm, I pulled it away from me and stood. Euphoric chills tickled up my spine as I stood and Mike's hand slid down my back and over my rump. The black dress I wore, the only one I owned, the one I'd worn when I made out with Cyrus for the first time, clung to my curves. The pounds I'd lost on my trip to hell had smoothed out my hips, and the dress fit perfectly. My black cardigan had a hole in the armpit, but the skinny straps on my dress weren't appropriate for both the weather and occasion. According to my mother. Tatum would have approved. Although she'd have insisted I wear anything but a pair of black on black sneakers. I'd run for my life too often in the recent weeks. The occult was no place for heels.

I hadn't really prepared anything substantial. The morning had mostly been spent watching Mike sleep and replaying all of my mistakes over and over in my head. And Crunch Berries. Mom hadn't questioned his presence when we both emerged from the bedroom for breakfast. She had, however, not stopped smiling until the moment we walked into the chapel.

"Good morning." My husky voice sounded more chipper than I'd intended. Clearing my throat, I locked eyes with Mike who squinted at me. "I hadn't really planned anything to say so this is going to be brief." I made eye contact with one of the press badge men. "For those of you who may not know me," *I killed the woman in this box I'm holding*, "my name is Dylan and Tatum was my best friend. For longer than I can remember, she and I have been inseparable." A knowing smile crept across my face as I faded into memory. "Literally, the Yin to my Yang, Tatum was always there to balance me out." *Liar*. "Ha, who am I kidding? If you're here because you knew Tatum Price personally,"—I locked eyes with the two press dudes—"you know she was the first one to push the envelope. If I wanted to have only a beer, she'd buy shots until two in the morning. If I thought some guy was cute,"—I looked at Mike and smiled, though Cyrus was the face running through my mind—"she'd do everything in her power to make sure I didn't chicken out."

Recalling the night she'd taken me to Macabre Saturnine, I stifled a laugh. She'd nearly shoved me into Cyrus's arms. Although she wasn't there the day I'd met Mike, she'd known from day one he and I were destined to be together. Cyrus was a good distraction from my gloomy post-Mike life, but when it came right down to it, Tatum would have slapped me silly if I never went back and made it work with Mike.

"So much like me in so many ways, she and I could quickly turn a good time into the need for bail money." I looked at Mike who was finally smiling with the memory of bailing us out of the clink. "In death, we always fluff the truth and forget most of what made that person human in the first place." *Don't forget my human when I'm gone,* I thought as I looked at Mike. "I could stand up here all day and tell Tatum tales, but each of you already have your own stories and memories." Mom sniffed back snot and began to quietly sob. Tatum had been as much of a daughter to her as I was for years after her parents died. "So I'll leave you with this." I stopped for a dramatic pause and to drum up something memorable and sincere. "Be excellent to each other." I stole a line from another bogus journey, and nobody was the wiser. "You never know when some asshole is going to come along and lop your head off." I shrugged. "Or try to anyway."

Everyone stared blankly at me. Except Dominika. Her smile spread from ear-to-ear. I'd left my bag of fucks in hell and had none to give my shocked audience. I was hurting more than any one of those assholes. Aside from Mom and Mike, not a one of them really knew Tatum. Not like I did. Even my hollow seemed to shut up and lie still to revel in the moment.

"Thanks for coming out," I said nervously, unsure of how to end my speech. Mom widened her eyes at me. "Oh, sorry, we will be meeting at La Grande on Mesa Vista for lunch right now. Uh, we'd really like to see you all there." With a nod, I closed it out and left the podium.

The preacher man shook my hand and blessed me and my soul. My darkness sneered from deep inside, and I jerked my hand away from him. The realization had come in slowly at first, then all at once. There was no denying it. Something had followed me home. The likelihood that something was the same something I'd been fighting for weeks was high. My little friend Angie wouldn't rest until I was finished with her.

"Remember what I said about public?" asked Mike.

I leaned in close. "I agreed with you." I'd said it so quietly I wondered if he'd even heard me as I walked past him.

"Well, well, Dylan, darling, you're just a little fat ball of badass, aren't you?" Dominika wrapped her slender arm around my shoulders with a smile.

Cyrus took both of my hands in his. "I'm sorry, but we won't make it to lunch." I figured as much. "Official business and all."

"How long will they be in town?" It had been a few days since I'd gotten word there was a cabal hullabaloo, and no new information had come to light.

He dropped his voice so no one could hear. "Too long."

"He's shaking in his boobs." Dominika snickered.

I couldn't figure out if her English mashed up every long o word with boobs or she just loved saying boobs. "I think you mean boots," I mumbled.

Cyrus closed his eyes and rubbed his temples. The passive boy in his man panties was gone, and it was apparent Primus Cyrus couldn't hack it in the grown-up game.

"Dominika, please?" Cyrus scolded, and Dominika pouted, pulling her arm off my shoulders.

"Fine. She stinks anyway." Dominika turned her nose up at me and stomped away, taking the arm of one of the men they'd brought with them.

Smelling my pits, I checked again for the illusive stench.

"Why can't I smell it?" Cyrus's eyes widened. "Look, I know this may come as a shock to you, but I've already figured out basically what's going on with me and what I need to do to stop it."

"Dylan, I'm sorry, but I don't think you can possib—"

"I've brought a bit of the otherworld back with me because some assholes put a demonic hit out on my ass and now I have to convince them to call it off. Or kill them."

"Well, that pretty much sums it up," he agreed.

Over his shoulder, I caught Mike watching every moment of the interaction, which was fine with me, but also watching were the two men in press badges.

"Go." I nodded toward the door and pushed at Cyrus. Mike caught on and followed. Outside and clear of prying ears, I continued. "I can feel it growing inside me," I said quickly before Mike found us. "One minute I'm me and the next I'm… not." He nodded, thinking on my words. "Blood. I've been craving blood and meat and," I lowered my voice to a breath, "sex."

"Yes, a beautiful service," Cyrus said suddenly.

I creased my brows a second before Mike's hand touched my back. "You ready to fill me in?" His voice was low to match mine. He knew all too well as an officer that the men standing in that tiny chapel were likely there to get the scoop.

I raised my brows slyly at Cyrus, and he nodded. I wasn't ready to tell Mike about the thing inside me. So far it'd been tame compared to what I knew my body and mind were capable of while under the control of something foreign. He'd know when he needed to. Until then, I couldn't risk him running to the fray and getting himself killed. *By me.*

"Cyrus is getting grilled by Marienne Poisson's minions." I

thumbed his direction. "Can't make it to lunch."

"Not minions. Cohorts." He let out a sigh that seemed too human for the likes of him. "If they're not satisfied, more will come. And more until another Malcolm McTavish takes what is rightfully mine."

Apathetically, Mike shrugged. "You gotta do what you gotta do." He pulled me in closer. "Will you be ready to head out in a minute?" I nodded. Cyrus met his eyes over my shoulder. They exchanged a moment I couldn't track before it was over. "See you, man." He left and found Mom standing on the few steps in front of the chapel.

"He doesn't know?" Cyrus leaned in close enough I smelled his aftershave. He searched my eyes. "Of course he doesn't." His long fingers stroked a chiseled jaw. "I understand you're trying to protect him, but there is no room for that now. You know better than anyone knowledge is dangerous. But there is a point you can no longer run, and knowledge is the only power you have." He wrapped a hand around my arm. "For his sake, don't wait too long. Without the help of Lupe, I'm of little use."

"Actually,"—I started, looking around for peepers—"I know how to stop it." *I hope*. "Can you meet me at Sween tomorrow morning?"

He stood up straight. "What are you scheming?"

"My own damn rescue." I planted my hands on my hips. My natural snark and the bitter darkness mingled inside. Soon, it would know what I was planning and who knew what it would do to stop me. "Are you in or not?"

His eyes moved to focus on something over my shoulder. "Is he?" He nodded toward Mike.

"Not yet. You're the only thing I have between me and

fucking hell, or whatever that place is. I don't know what this is growing inside me, but it's scaring the fuck out of him. I'm scaring him. I'll be honest, I'm not sure I hate this kind of power. And that scares me more than anything. I need you. Please." I hated to beg, but my life was at stake. And with Mike back in the picture, I had a life worth living.

"Of course." He closed his eyes and shook his head. "We need to talk but not here. Come to Embrace this evening, before full dark. They'll be out until then."

Assuming he was talking about the southern cabal folks, I nodded my understanding. "I promise you won't have to kill anybody." Behind my back, I crossed my fingers.

"Yes. I'll bring Dominika." It was the last thing I would have requested, but her ruthlessness could come in handy. Specifically with regard to killing the one thing neither he nor Mike, no matter what they said, could kill. Me.

"Thank you." I knew what he meant and appreciated the forethought. I'd already taken Tatum. There was no telling what I was capable of. We couldn't risk me on the loose.

"Be safe. Will you? Keep Mike close by. He keeps you grounded."

His words reminded me of Lupe's spell before she dropped the chair. She'd sealed my verve with his blood, binding us together. I hadn't considered it before, but thanks to Lupe, Mike truly may have been my only salvation. He didn't know it yet, but he very well could have been the only reason I came back from the dead.

"More than you think." My smile fell flat.

The hollow space within lay dormant after unleashing a bit of aggression in the chapel. It seemed if I left it be, it left me be. Mostly. All I needed were food and sex to stay sane for twenty-four hours, until hopefully, the curator of my beasty came close enough to snarl in my trap.

Food and sex to stay alive for one more day.

Pity party is at five. BYOB.

ELEVEN

LUNCH WAS DELICIOUS. DRINKS WERE BETTER. MARGARITAS were not my usual drink of choice, but when sharing a few pitchers between me and Mom, I wasn't complaining. Drunk by three in the afternoon, even better. Only Mom and Mike made it to lunch, which was fine with me. The pressmen had actually been friends of Tatum's who'd come to pay their last respects. And probably also to get a scoop before the last of the untimely death of Tatum Price fizzled out completely, but they were kind enough to keep that to themselves. It may have been my chopping heads off reference that did it.

The three of us chatted about movies and television. Hardly mentioning Tatum. Mom didn't ask about Tahoe, which was surprising; her being her. She seemed happy enough with our current situation. Maybe she thought we'd work it out in the end. I hoped she was right.

Mike dumped off Mom and me before dusk. He'd insisted we come home with him, and I drunkenly explained we weren't that kind of family. He didn't think it was as funny as Mom did. Food and booze seemed to do the trick because I'd felt mostly normal all afternoon. For a moment, I wondered if I had overreacted and I truly would get better like Lupe said. She was, however, notoriously full of shit, so there really was no telling.

"I'll be back later," Mike said through his passenger window.

"You don't have to stay here."

He laughed condescendingly. "Yes, I do. Spend some time with your mom. I'm going to go feed the cat and take out the trash."

Normal shit for a normal dude. "You got it, Hoss." I saluted him, stumbling away from the car. I'd sobered up enough to drive nearly an hour before we left the restaurant, but he didn't need to know that. For all he knew, I was going inside to sleep it off. I had other plans.

Mom flopped on the recliner in front of the TV. "I'm so full." She rubbed her belly. "Nap time." Her giggle faded as she closed her eyes.

"Sweet. See ya." I kissed her on the forehead, swiping her car keys on the way to the door. "I'll be back in an hour."

"Where you headed?"

"Gotta see a man about a thing." I skirted around the question.

"Have fun doing that." Her slurs made me laugh.

I closed the front door halfway and stopped. "Hey,"—I stepped back in—"no match dot com while I'm gone. You're too drunk for that shit." It was her favorite drunk hobby. Checking out dudes she'd never date in the light of day. I had to explain too many times if their profile picture was them with their Harley, it wasn't a good match.

Mom waved her hand sloppily as I shut the door. Scanning the street for Mike, I felt guilt creep up from somewhere deep in the recesses hidden away beyond the hollow. It was stupid to lie that late in the game. He'd know sooner or later if he didn't already have some kind of suspicion.

Though the current situation was extraordinary to say the least, it was no different than it had always been with him, how I'd always felt I needed to be. Normal. And if I wasn't normal, I faked it. Not well and usually I didn't care one way or the other, but feigning normalcy kept the status quo, and that made it worth it. Pretending to be something you're not was exhausting. Hypocrisy being one of my pet peeves, pretending to be a regular girl got old fast. He'd never felt safe with me out in the world. As though I would suddenly combust while waiting in the drive-thru or something.

I couldn't live under his thumb then, just as I couldn't with a beasty residing inside me. The only difference being I didn't know what I wanted then. The probability of losing everything put things into perspective and made it clear in my head where I belonged. He'd come around as well and soon, he would either have to accept the world and me for what we were, or get lost. Inwardly, I hoped he was strong enough to see me through it, because unlike then, I needed him. I was quickly losing myself, and the only person I trusted to bring me back was Michael Petersen.

It was dark by the time I pulled into the parking lot down the street from Embrace. The street was loaded with cars, and the venue itself provided little parking. People milled around the other bars and establishments in the area. Some looked as though they were also heading toward Embrace, while everyone else moved dramatically out of the way when the innocent little vamp kids passed them. Shaking my head, I laughed to myself as I too passed, but no one moved for me. Little did they know I was the monster they should've feared. Unassuming, normal little fat girl, no one was the wiser. My beasty sure picked a good hiding spot to lie in wait.

The man at the door nodded at me as he moved the velvet rope. The days of signing in, dudes in tiny black T-shirts, and formalities were over. I was officially a regular. Or I had otherworldly being tattooed across my forehead.

Or on my arm.

Darkened space, lit primarily by candlelight, it took almost a full minute for my eyes to adjust to the lighting. Still in my black dress and sneakers, I didn't exactly fit in with the macabre vampy patrons that filled the place. It wasn't anything new. Perhaps that was what drew me to that crowd in the first place. It was the only time I actually felt somewhat normal and utterly abnormal in the same instant.

"Drink?" Dominika suddenly stood in front of me, holding a beverage in my face.

"Probably a good idea." I took the glass from her hand without question. I stopped a moment before the liquid hit my lips, eyeing the contents. She'd never welcomed me with such vigor before. "This clean?" I suspiciously pointed a single finger at the glass.

"Yes," Dominika said, rolling her eyes and slouching her shoulders. "Boring," she said under her breath.

"You standing here with a drink at the ready tells me Cyrus is otherwise occupied." My drink disappeared down my gullet before she had a chance to take a breath.

A slight shift of her eyes and nod pointed out Cyrus chatting with a petite woman and large bearded man near the bar.

"Shit, I thought I'd beat them here. It's not that dark out yet." I examined the bottom of my empty glass. "I take it this is some serious shit."

She tilted her head nonchalantly and shrugged. "He brought it on himself."

"Is he in some kind of trouble for… what happened?" *Because technically,* you *killed their Primus. But that's none of my business.*

"Isn't he always?" She turned away from me to eye the crowd.

"I really wouldn't know." Our relationship hadn't moved beyond the awkward 'running for your life' phase.

I just met you and this is crazy, but there's some dead girls and headless ladies.

"Oh? Shouldn't you?"

"How the hell do you figure that?"

She laughed, throwing her head back. "Dear, Donnie." She patted me on the head while I fumed. "That boy has been trouble from day one. Too human to play vampire. I figured a woman of your prowess could have discovered that by now."

"What else is the guy supposed to do with his eternal life? I mean, who else is he supposed to hang with?"

She moved her face closer to mine, looking deep into my eyes. "He should have died a century ago. House of Sandorus should have never fallen. This,"—she looked around with disdain—"this is a joke."

"You really don't have to—" Cyrus yelled after the petite woman as she headed my direction.

"Dylan Hart, I presume." She stuck her small hand out not

for me to shake but to kiss.

Scoffing quietly, I took her hand firmly in mine and gave it an All-American two-pump. "Ma'am."

"Genevieve Poisson."

"Poisson?" I let my expression do the talking.

"Dylan," Cyrus said breathlessly, panting after his sprint. "This is Primus, House of Porte. Marienne's oldest sister."

"Sister?" I raised my brows and eyed the woman in front of me. Their family resemblance lacking, I recognized her as the woman in white lace I'd dined with in New Orleans. Marienne's Secondus.

"*Qui*," she said curtly. "I understand you lost a dear friend in our city."

"I did," I replied, not allowing sadness to reach my voice.

"On behalf of Porte and the southern cabal, my condolences to you. As you know, we lost our dear Primus as well."

I eyed Cyrus who nodded. "I did hear something like that. I'm sorry. Those d'Entremontes—"

"d'Entremonte?" Genevieve pulled her expertly plucked eyebrows in together. Cyrus took in a gulp of air and stepped back.

"Uh, yeah. You know, Azelie and Zoran. You know… right?"

"Miss Poisson, my office is just around back if you wouldn't mind—"

"I do very much mind. What is this?" She held her hand out to me as though someone had attempted to serve her a Big Mac at a five star restaurant.

Cyrus, at a loss for words, stared at the woman. The large man stood resigned behind her. His piercing blue eyes burrowed into me. His long black beard reminded me of the man I'd thought looked so much like Rasputin while at the House of

Porte. Likely it was the same man. Many of those faces I'd long forgotten and replaced with the images of far more terrifying individuals.

"Azelie d'Entremonte and her brother Zoran killed Malcolm, Marienne, and our friend Tatum Price." They all stared at me. "I think," I added quickly, removing myself from the night in question.

"I believe your office is a better place for this discussion." Her eyes never left me. Brows pulled together, she finally looked as old as her aging sister, but not *older*.

"This way." Cyrus turned and led the way. Dominika and the House of Porte people followed.

"Miss Hart?" Genevieve called over her shoulder when I didn't move.

"Me?" I asked, looking around to be sure.

"You seem to be the only honest person here."

Welcome to the club.

I figured by honest she meant stupid. Cyrus and his diplomacy had fucked up his situation for him, and my mouth made it worse.

"I'm nobody."

She stepped closer to me so only I could hear her words. "The odor of death is upon you. A human soul transitioning from the otherworld? You are quite certainly somebody." She looked me up and down. "From what I can see, more than one." Turning on a heel, she followed Cyrus and didn't look back.

Not knowing if she referred to my demonic stowaway or made a jab at my girth, I scowled behind her back. With no weapon to speak of—having left my only gun at Sween and tucking Tatum's knife under my mattress—I thought twice about following three vampires and one century-old human-lion guy to a secluded room. I checked Mom's phone for the time and figured I had about an hour before Mike would be heading back to Mom's. If I wasn't there, he'd come looking. That fact I could take to the bank. A thick shoulder slammed into me on my way to certain death. Icy liquid spilled down the center of my cleavage.

"Oh, oh, shit. I'm so sorry." The stocky blond Sam-replacement, Luke, apologized profusely, hands full of half-empty glasses.

"Since when did security work the floor?"

"We're short-staffed tonight. Head cheese said these visitors were some corporate bigwigs and we had to run like a well-oiled machine." He leaned in closer. "Between you and me, those two don't look like corporate people at all."

I laughed, wiping away booze from my boobs. "You have no idea." I patted him on the shoulder. "Next time, aim for my mouth." Realizing the context of my words could have been misconstrued as something far more perverted than booze, I changed the subject and scurried away. "Keep your nose clean, kid," I shouted over my shoulder, leaving him with his hands full. He'd learn the ropes soon enough, and before long, he'd be just as corrupt as I was.

The vampire people and Cyrus had disappeared out the door by the time I got there. The clanging metal steps still echoed through the alley when I opened the back door. The train of Dominika's dress disappeared, and the door slammed shut.

A howling gust whistled through the narrow space, kicking up trash and flitting it through the air. Misty November fog hovered above puddles of water. My brain told me the scene should be terrifying and on the surface, I was scared. The hairs on my arms stood on end, stomach tingling with intuitive fear.

But at the core, deep down where it counted, I didn't think I felt anything at all. The hollow swallowed my human fears and left me feeling nothing.

I clambered up the steps, making more noise than I would have liked. Swinging open the door without knocking, I startled everyone inside. They all turned to face me, expressionless. As though they had all been sitting in suspended animation until the moment I opened the door.

"Hey." I waved, not moving my hand past my hip. The last place I wanted to be was trapped in a room full of vampires out for blood, with a devil on my back. But, there I was. "What's up?"

The Moroccan office I remembered was gone, and an understated masculine décor had taken its place. The brightly colored carpet and drapes had been replaced with archaic paintings of war and an oversized animal hide rug. A large cherry wood desk sat in the center surrounded by cushy leather chairs. The space looked more intended for Malcolm than Cyrus. Exuding masculinity wasn't ever Cyrus's strong suit. In fact, the more I got to know him, the more I came to realize he really didn't know what the fuck he was doing. The memories of Cy-bot, human cyborg underwear model, had long since passed. I wondered if that had ever truly been him in the first place. Endearing and compassionate, his demeanor didn't fool me. I knew deep down in there, Cyrus would trade me in for his own life any day of the week. Hell, he said it himself. I'd have found someone who would. I could only assume he was referring to dying and that *someone* he referred to was Mike.

"Please have a seat," said the petite Primus.

Genevieve controlled the room with nothing more than her presence. Like her sister, the power that rolled off her filled the room and demanded your attention. The Rasputin guy stood behind her chair watching over everyone. Dominika leaned against the wall behind Cyrus, where he sat at his desk, looking bored as usual.

"Can't stay long. I've got a friend waiting in the car." I preempted, referring to Tatum's box. "What is it you need from me?" Though her power was strong, my empty core didn't have time for fear, and I ignored the prickling awareness creeping up my spine.

Genevieve cocked a tawny brow in my direction. "More than I believe you can provide, but for now, I would like to hear how you came about visiting our little town last month."

Referring to New Orleans as a little town was like referring to my ass as a bit plump. Understatement to say the least. "An invitation from the late Primus, Malcolm McTavish and then Secondus, Cyrus Atossa."

"She attended as my escort," Cyrus butted in.

Genevieve shot him a glare and he backed down. Playing boss man may have been proving too much for the not-so-vampire boy.

"What he said." I nodded in Cyrus's direction. "During my visit, I met and instantly enraged Azelie d'Entremonte. She spent the rest of the weekend tormenting me until I fled your little town for my life. When I returned…" I stopped and thought about my words. "They were all dead."

Genevieve nodded sympathetically. Still, it was likely she was just as full of shit as I was.

"You did not witness Azelie murder my sister?" I shook my head emphatically. It wasn't a lie because she didn't really do it. Dominika didn't move a muscle as she leaned against the wall. Her moral compass only pointed south. "What makes you so sure she is our culprit?"

"Crystal ball," I answered facetiously. "Can I go? I really do have somewhere to be." *Jeopardy* was on in fifteen minutes.

"Not yet." She flipped her hand in my direction instructing me to park my butt back in the seat. "If you believe so wholeheartedly Azelie d'Entremonte killed your friend, why have you not gone to the police with this information?"

My palms began sweating under the leather arms of the chair. Cyrus eyed me cautiously. Dominika didn't give a shit either way. Rasputin stared a hole through my head. Genevieve's honey brown eyes looked at me softly. She didn't need intimidation to force information from my mouth. All she needed was to ask.

"Because I killed her," I blurted out. Genevieve nodded slightly as though she already knew, but Rasputin appeared enraged. "I lopped the bitch's head off. She can't hurt anyone again."

Everyone was quiet. Genevieve's soft features didn't move an inch. Not a wrinkle on her face, I found it hard to believe she was Marienne's older sister. Dominika said they aged at a much slower rate than humans, but never mentioned anything about slower than each other.

"If you want more than that, you'll have to kill me because I'm taking that story to my grave. Just know your sister was ass deep in magic and mayhem and basically got herself killed."

Letting out a feminine sigh, Genevieve leaned back into her chair. The look of annoyance passed over her face. "She wanted a little one in the house. I could not understand why anyone would ever willingly bring a screaming beast into their home, but the urge drove her nearly to the brink of insanity."

"I knew it," I exclaimed loudly and slapped my hand against

the leather arm.

"As her Secondus, the madness was too much to bear. Why she would choose a child over her youth I will never know." She ran a delicate hand over her cheek. "Involving the d'Entremontes was a mistake from the beginning, but Marienne swore she knew what she was doing." The mundane tone of her voice made it seem as though she was talking about why anyone would own a pit bull instead of the deadly subject at hand. "House of Porte has never played well with the magical people of New Orleans, and over the years, those two nearly lost their heads more than once at the hands of a Porte member. It was bound to happen, I suppose." She looked at her own nails, examining them nonchalantly.

My jaw fell to my chest. Eyes sliding to Cyrus for an explanation, his expression matched mine. A simple, straightforward explanation of events was nearly unheard of when it came to those people. If only Cyrus and Malcolm had been so forthcoming, I might not have been holding back a creeping darkness from engulfing me completely.

"Close your mouth, sweetie, you will catch flies, as they say."

I snapped it shut duly. "So," my voice cracked and I cleared my throat, "you and Marienne collected blood with Azelie and Zoran?"

"Oh, gods no." I let out a sigh. If Genevieve was a part of it all, then that meant it wasn't over. Not by a long shot. "I am a busy girl, you know, I have no time for collecting. However, the benefits are glorious." A statement made obvious by her youthful appearance.

Cyrus remained silent, seemingly as astonished as I was. Even Dominika seemed more interested in the conversation since Genevieve's revelation.

"Where did Azelie come in?" I asked, hoping her flow of information didn't stop.

"You have many questions."

"Yeah, they rarely get answered." I shot Cyrus a look from the corner of my eye.

She tilted her head and looked me up and down. "Or perhaps you've asked the wrong questions." She turned to Cyrus. "Mr. Atossa, I am disappointed in you. Look what has become of the poor girl." She fanned her hand toward me. Her head turned quickly and her eyes met mine. "When you play in the darkness, you bring home the shadows, little one."

"Duly noted." Leaning forward and pulling her attention toward me, I kicked myself for not bringing my trusty bag inside with me. I really could have used a tape recorder. Shit, even a pen and paper would have helped. Begging my brain to function, I thought of the most important questions I'd yet to find answers to. "Here's a question for you. If Marienne hired Azelie to collect the blood—I'm assuming here, so correct me if I'm wrong—and put some kind of magical mojo on it to keep it fresh, who killed Regina and the other eight girls since May?"

She shifted uncomfortably in her chair. The first human movement I'd seen her make. Touching the hand of Rasputin, she turned over her shoulder. "Get me a drink?" she whispered.

He followed orders and cautiously moved past me and out the door. His eyes remained trained on me the whole way there.

"Curious little one," she said to Cyrus.

He closed his eyes and sighed. "You have no idea."

"Well, humph, it's no wonder you are in the situation you are. You know what they say about curiosity?"

"Fuck that cat. Answer my question." The dark hollow rumbled. "Who's beheading these girls?" The fact that she was avoiding the question told me she had something to hide.

Shrugging lightly, the motion was sexier than it should have been. "Why would you think I would have any information about some dead girls?"

"Because one of them for sure was working directly for Azelie and thus for your sister." I pointed to her face. "Judging by that mug, you've been reaping the benefits of that business transaction. That makes you an accomplice in the very least." Instantly, I wished Mike had been there to hit her with the law, but he'd have just made things worse in the long run. "If you're anything like these guys," I thumbed in the direction of the vampire people, "I can safely assume you don't want the law snooping around your sanctuary." Leaning on the edge of my seat, I did my best Mike impersonation. "It's best if you just come clean now. I can keep you safe if you can just help me out." Good cop Mike.

"Ha!" She laughed, boisterous and unattractive. "You think *you* can protect *me*?"

"From the law?" I nodded. "I could also have a gaggle of swat officers beating down your door by midnight. I'd hate to know what you've got locked away in that big old house." I lowered my voice. "Blood doesn't wash away like you might think." I'd seen the stains around the drain in the basement firsthand. I sat back in my seat, folding my hands in my lap. "Your choice." Bad cop Mike.

A long pause stretched out between us. Her eyes moved slowly to Cyrus. "Your cabal should be unsanctioned. The only soul in this room qualified to lead is Dominika." Obviously flustered, Genevieve searched for words. "Two humans, cursed to live out their days trapped halfway between this world and the next. Your immortality will not buy our loyalty. Nicolas is dead. His wishes died with him."

"He was murdered," Cyrus said under his breath, staring at the top of his desk. "His wishes are his legacy. I am his legacy."

"You are a joke." She stood. "You sit in this place, you watch your little groupies as they writhe on one another, trick them with Hollywood magic and drugs, and you call it art. All the while raking in the profits of their stupidity. This is a disgrace."

He shook his head. "Not me. Not Nicolas. Malcolm McTavish created this… empire." Cyrus clenched his fists, knuckles turning white.

"And here you are. Malcolm is dead, and just like Nicolas decreed, you have taken your throne. You were a pathetic man passing as a beautiful untouchable, and now…" Genevieve waved her hand as if to showcase his riches. "Perhaps it was not Azelie who murdered our dear friends after all."

"Malcolm McTavish took my throne when he murdered Nicolas in cold blood." His revelation brought my shocked eyebrows to my hairline.

"And rightfully so. Nicolas lost his mind when he created you. His eternal pet."

"He loved me." Cyrus stood and slammed his fists against the tabletop. "Nicolas Sandorus was a legend. A hero to many. A hero to me. He saved my people. He saved *me*." His voice cracked with the threat of tears. Silently, I rooted for him to hold it together long enough to show that bitch what for.

"He cursed you, fool." Genevieve stepped closer to Cyrus. Power rolled through the room like an electrical current. "His selfishness abounded, he cursed you to live for eternity by his side. He didn't love you. He coveted you."

Cyrus's chest heaved with heavy breaths. "Your murderous sister took Malcolm's head out of spite." He stepped close to her, towering over her petite frame. "We burned them to ashes and left it for the birds to peck at. You want your inquest? Here it is." He stood a foot taller than her, but you'd never notice the difference in their power. "Fuck off. This is my town. My cabal. I am Primus House of Sandorus." *Throwback cabal.* "I banish you and your house from dealings with the Western Cabal. You will cease all illegal activity immediately or face the consequences. Age gracefully or not at all."

My eyes shot back and forth between them. Vampire battle royale unfolding before my eyes.

Genevieve turned her soft face up to him. "Ask Malcolm who killed Regina," she said softly. "Oh, I'm sorry." She feigned remorse. "You can't." She moved toward the door. "What do you do with a horse when it's no longer useful?" Her eyes slid to Dominika as she cocked a brow.

The door opened, and Rasputin stood there with a drink in his hand. Genevieve took it and swigged it back. "Be seeing you, little one." She winked at me and ushered her bearded boy out the door.

Glass shattered against the metal staircase as the door shut. "Those glasses are not cheap." Dominika stood up straight and glared at the door.

Astonished at the power play I'd just witnessed, I couldn't figure out what to say first. "That's what you're concerned about? Glassware?"

Cyrus flopped into his seat and held his head in his hands. His breaths came fast, too fast. If he'd been mostly human, I'd have said he was on his way to hyperventilating.

"Dominika, can you get him something to drink?" She

looked shocked. "I won't tell anyone you did something nice for me. He needs a minute and an alcoholic beverage." I let my shoulders slump. "Please."

Rolling her eyes, she stormed out the door and clomped loudly down the steps. I wrapped my arms around his shoulders. The dark hollow in me enjoyed his scent, and I silently rejoiced in the sensation of holding him close.

Shaking his head, he whispered, "He loved me. He didn't do this to me. He couldn't."

"Actually," the hollow spoke for me, "I think he did. That's what Dominika said anyway." My nonchalant tone brought his attention to me. His green eyes met mine, hurt filled them to brim with tears. "Sorry. Someone should have told you sooner."

He scoffed, shooting snot from his nose. "Yes, they should have." His breaths slowed as he searched my eyes. "Why are you only telling me now? You've been a trustworthy ally, why keep this from me?" Tears wet his lashes but didn't fall.

I searched the hollow for an answer but got nothing in return. "No need to hurt you now after all these years."

"Indeed." He turned his chair to face me. "Trust Dylan Hart to destroy centuries-old belief." I shrugged. What else could I do? Genevieve had beckoned the beast, and now it sat in wait, wrath unfulfilled, no food to satiate its hunger. Apathy would take over until the beast was free to run amuck. "Why must we cling to false truths?"

"I do believe it's part of the human condition."

He wrapped long fingers around my biceps and pulled me down closer to him. "I don't mean to alarm you, but I'm afraid you have a visitor." His eyes penetrated mine, seeing something I only felt inside.

He was wholly and unequivocally correct. I drew in his

scent. Skin, sweat, centuries-old blood coursing through his veins. Leaning in, I touched my lips lightly over his. "I know." He breathed softly. "Whatever will we do about this?"

He pressed his mouth to mine gently. "Someone really should have told you sooner." He pulled away from me. "Time is your enemy. The longer it festers in your sorrow, the stronger it will become."

Breaths came shallow, pulsing through my nose. Beastly hunger rolled inside, pleading for my sins to keep it still.

"Every minute that passes I feel the hollow growing. Sins and sorrow fuel it. Blood and sex keep it at bay. At times, I can't seem to control my own body and others, I'm perfectly fine." Its claws ticked up from the depths. "I'm holding on, but I don't know how much longer before I can't anymore. I could live with this inside me forever if I knew the outcome wasn't deadly." I spoke quickly, forcing the words out of my mouth before something else took control. "There is only one consensus as to how to make this stop. Find the source and kill it. I fear this thing inside me knows what I'm planning and is lying in wait for me to give up. I won't. Not yet. Not when there's so much to lose." Cyrus was quiet, contemplative. "Meet me at Sween tomorrow at eight in the morning." I kissed him one more time before I stood. I needed to move away from him. The hunger was beginning to gain ground in his scent.

"Where are you going?" he asked as I walked to the door.

"I gotta call a guy about some dead girls." I smiled over my shoulder. "Don't worry. I got this." I moved my hand over my center where I felt the beast was hiding. "Keep your phone on you just in case," I said as the door shut behind me.

Dominika slinked up the stairs, drinks in hand. "Where are you off to?"

"Like you care." I scoffed as I passed her.

She grabbed my arm, squeezing tightly. "I know the feeling

of void indifference. Void is hundreds of years on the earth. Hiding in the shadows. Fearing your own willpower. Void is the hollow inside when there is nothing left to feel but the decay of your own body. I warned you so many months ago. I told you what we are and what we are capable of. I feel you're now capable of much worse." Her eyes slid up and down me. "Could be fun. But for your own sake, do not allow the hollow to consume you." She raised a brow and released me. "Then you'll be just like me." Her cobalt blue eyes glistened with what I thought might be tears. "Rotten," she whispered.

Her heels clanked against the stairs as she ascended. "And what was your warning?" I recalled Cyrus pulling me frantically through the crowds of Embrace toward the very stairs we stood upon while the Hungarian screamed across the room in a language I didn't understand.

Stopping at the door, she balanced glasses in one hand. "I will eat your heart while you sleep," she said with a sultry grin.

I nodded, and the door slammed shut. "Yeah, that's about what I thought." I also agreed with her. I was totally capable of that and more should the beast within get its claws in deep enough.

I had a little over twelve hours to keep my beast at bay until my chance would come to kill it for good. If Angie wouldn't meet me, I'd come to her. With a vengeance.

Hitting speed dial, the phone rang on the other end. "Meet me at Mom's. I've got something I know you're going to want to hear," I said to the man on the other line.

I will eat you while you sleep.

TWELVE

“YOU HAVE GOT TO BE FUCKING KIDDING ME!” I BELLOWED as the front door slammed shut behind me.

My mom sat stone silent in the recliner. Glistening brown eyes were wide and filled with terrified tears. Her hands bound together at her wrists. A dirty sock shoved in her mouth. At her throat, a long sharp blade straight out of a Renaissance Faire. Trembling fingers gripped the handle. Dirty fingernails and track marks up her arm let me know Angie hadn’t been doing so hot since I’d last seen her.

“You shut your fat face, bitch. Shut it,” she screeched. Her adorable pixie face was nearly a ghost of what it once was. Drawn cheeks and sunken eyes accentuated her pointed chin. Her hand shook violently as it held the knife to Mom’s throat.

“Fat face? Is that the best you can do?”

"Terry," she said, looking toward the TV which I couldn't see from my place at the front door. "Get her."

"Get her?" I quoted Bill Murray and dropped my bag to the ground. My fingers laced well between my keys. "You should know, I've killed things uglier than you." It was a lie, Azelie was anything but ugly, and the demon thing didn't seem too dead to me, but Terry didn't need to know that.

Ruddy skin and acne proved he and Angie had probably shared a pipe a time or two. A set of tweakers with Satan and vengeance on their side, as if my life needed anything more ridiculous.

Mike was on his way. It couldn't be too long before he'd be walking in the door behind me. I only had to fend them off long enough for the fuzz to bust in and break up the shenanigans.

"You killed Zeph." Terry sneered.

I laughed. "Technically—"

"Shut up!" Angie pressed the blade against Mom's throat. Mom swallowed hard, the blade bobbed. Her face passive, she sat motionless, not comprehending what was happening around her.

"Look, I'm sorry your friend died." I stalled. "But really, I didn't do anything to him. His own grandma… well…" I slid my finger across my throat dramatically. "Sad really. Her own grandson." Slowly, I'd moved a few steps closer to Angie. Terry flanked me, but didn't seem to notice my movement. "I had no idea of course." Play innocent. Step forward. "My life was at stake. Zephyrinus was payment for my remedy. That's why I called you. You see, I couldn't live with myself these last few weeks. Had I known…?" I shook my head and stepped forward.

"Stop. Just stop it." Angie shook. Her irrational meth high had brought her to my home, but that wouldn't last, and soon there would be a conscience behind that gaunt face, and the girl holding a knife to my mother would either be dead or in prison.

The honest part of me didn't know which I cared to have.

I raised my hands in surrender. "I just want to talk to you." *How the fuck did you find my mom's house?* My tone slipped into a slithering aura of manipulation. "Angela, listen, I know what you're going through." I just needed to get close enough to take that knife. Mom eyed me cautiously. An empty set of beer bottles sat beside her on the table. "I just buried my best friend. Well, not buried. She's in my bag."

Angie's brows pulled in at the center, and Terry scoffed.

"No really. She's in my bag." I watched Terry over my shoulder as I moved closer. "Don't believe me? Check for yourself."

He met Angie's eyes. A quick nod and he was off digging through the bag I'd dropped to the floor in anger. Angie watched him intently. Her drug-fueled brain couldn't track Terry and me at the same time.

More quickly than I thought possible, I lunged toward her. Clawing her ghostlike face with my keys. She screamed and swung the blade away from Mom and toward me. Cutting deep across my forearm, the blade fileted my skin apart like a fish. One swift movement a moment sooner and Mom would have been toast.

Terry turned toward the commotion. Tatum's black plastic box in his hands. The bronze urn would take three to four weeks for delivery. He stood in awe. Not prepared to go down in a blaze of glory, he dropped Tatum to the tile and scurried out the front door. Leaving it open behind him.

Angie stumbled into me, knife held above my head. Speckles of blood oozed from her cheek where my keys had scratched across it. Grabbing her arm with both hands, I pushed against her. Weight on my side, I shoved as hard as I could. She lost her step and stumbled back into the china hutch. Glass clattered behind her as one of Grandma's dishes tumbled over.

"That was an heirloom," I growled, repeating my mother's words from many moments in my childhood. A headbutt sent the back of her head into the wooden edge of the hutch and her eyes crossed. The dark hollow returned and brought with it a sneer of contention. "You did this to me." I held up my arm brandishing the devilish tattoo that had appeared overnight. "How?" I asked, clasping my hand around her throat. "How do I stop it? How do I get rid of this thing?" I growled.

Angie's eyes became saucers as she looked at me. "What *are* you?" Fear dripped off her like sweat on a humid day. The scent was intoxicating.

"You tell me. Day after day this thing festers inside me. Growing stronger. Calling me out and forcing me into submission. I know you sent this thing to me, now call it off. I'm sorry your friend is dead but a lot more people, innocent people, are going to die if you don't make this stop." I eyed Mom who stared at me in horror. I hadn't been prepared for Angie, but there she was, and I was going to get the most from it.

"I didn't—" She shook her head repeatedly.

"Bullshit." I pushed my palm into her throat drawing from her a high-pitched squeal. Breaths pulsed through my nostrils.

One solid jolt, more pressure, a spare moment to a let loose the beast, and she'd have been dead. I snarled and pushed just a little harder.

"No, no." She choked. "I did. Okay, I did." Tears fell down her sunken cheeks. "You deserved vengeance, and we reaped it." Her voice was a strangled whisper. "Together we joined in summoning Ashmedai to torment you as retribution for Zephyrinus." Her eyes slid to the dark black ink on my arm. "That is his mark." Her eyes flicked from mine to my arm and back again, seeing something in them that terrified her. "I can't… I can't do *that*."

"Then who?" I barked and shoved my thick body against hers.

Shaking her head, she cried, unable to speak properly with my hand around her throat. I released her and held tight to her shirt instead. "I don't know how this happened. Possession is rare. A vessel must be wide open for him to take hold. For a demon to manifest and take over a human soul…" The corners of her mouth turned down. "There's something wrong with you." She shook her head until I thought it was going to spin off her shoulders.

Wrong with me*?* "Stop shaking your fucking head and talk to me." I shook her by the collar of her plaid shirt. "Tough guy can't handle a little bit of hell?" A smile cocked the side of my mouth. "You wanted damnation, baby, here it is." I slid my face closer to hers until our noses touched. "Eat your heart out." My voice a warbled gurgle, the voice of my demon passenger growled at the girl. I pulled her terrified scent in deep through my nose. It tugged at those same tingly bits Mike and Cyrus had. "Or I could." My voice, a garbled version of my own, was nearly a replica of the black beasty I'd followed to the otherworld in search of Tatum.

"Hey, hands up," Mike yelled from behind me.

My beast slithered home at the sound of his voice. I sucked in one last breath of her and peered innocently over my shoulder. Terry sat cuffed on the floor by the door. Panting, Mike pulled his blazer off and tossed it on Mom's couch. He hadn't changed since he dropped us off.

"I'm sorry. I'm sorry." Angie's voice trembled.

Knuckles white, I loosened my grip and straightened her shirt.

"Mom," Mike called out and ran to her.

Pulling the sock from her mouth, he looked her over for injuries. A bright red streak marred her throat. Eyes wide, terror hiding around the edges. "I'm fine," she whispered as Mike untied her wrists.

"I'm calling a bus." He pulled his phone from his pocket and called for an ambulance. He hadn't paid much attention to Angie and me as he focused on what he viewed as the top priority in the room. For once, I felt Mike knew I could handle myself. Oddly, in the moment, I absolutely was not handling anything.

Angie slid to the floor and huddled around her knees. Whatever she'd seen in me scared the fuck out of her. She went from tweak to timid in two seconds flat. Lupe promised it would go away, Dominika said I stank of hell, and Cyrus seemed more concerned for me than ever before. Regardless of who or how, I wanted it the fuck out of me. I also kind of wanted bacon.

"I'm not going to the hospital." Mom was adamant.

"Dylan—"

"Yes, you are. You'll go, you'll get some rest, and you'll come home tomorrow morning." Mike would win. He always did. Mom wasn't as willful as I was. I took after my dad in that aspect.

"Fine. But I'm not staying. There's no reason. I really am fine." The beer clung to her breath. Mike noticed the bottles too and shot me a look. She'd been almost out when I left her. More alcohol meant she had been pretty well gone when Angie and Terry showed up. It didn't look like there'd been a struggle before I got there. If she hadn't been mostly drunk, who knows what could have happened to her.

Warm blood dripped down my arm from the gash I'd received at the hand of Angie. Adrenaline and my dark hollow had blocked out the pain, and I hadn't even noticed the mess I'd been making with it until Mike's eyes fell over the red splatters on the carpet.

Quickly, he grabbed my arm. "You're hurt pretty bad," he pointed out and held my arm up for me to see. "She did this to you?" he asked, nodding at Angie who remained no threat as she huddled on the floor. I bobbed my head and scowled at the girl. "Wait here, I'll get you something to help that." He held my arm up above my head and motioned for me to keep it there while he disappeared into the kitchen.

A moment later, he returned. I was more than a little disappointed when I saw his help was in the form of a washcloth instead of an icy beer. I'd have preferred the beer. He pressed it hard against my arm and held it there for a few long, silent moments until backup arrived. Only the quiet sounds of Angie's sobs and the quick, rapid breaths from Mike were to be heard.

Before long, the familiar whoop of a police siren echoed through the neighborhood. A few heartbeats later, red and blue lights flashed from outside. Creating quite the spectacle, cops and paramedics parked along the street, blocking driveways and filling living rooms with their flashing lights. Radio chatter interrupted the quiet November night as too many cops milled around. It was a miracle what could happen when a fellow officer called in the heavies.

"What the hell is going on here?" Mike asked after Mom was out of earshot on a stretcher and in the ambulance.

I shook my head. "You literally do not want to know." He glared at me. "Two words: plausible deniability." I raised my eyebrows.

He closed his eyes slowly and shook his head. "Please tell me you didn't kill anyone."

"Not this time." *Not yet.*

He rubbed his forehead. "So what you're trying to tell me is these two broke into your house and held your mother hostage because of who you are as a person?"

"Basically."

"You're going to get me fired."

"Not today." I leaned in close to him. "All you need to know is that woman, just like Azelie, supremely fucked me." I tapped my evil ink. "I can't shake it without her, so it's a damn good thing she showed up on my doorstep. Or whatever." Standing on my tiptoes, I wrapped a gentle hand around his cheek and whispered into his ear. "I won't be pressing charges." I turned away. "I'll be needing her in one piece and as soon as possible."

I left him standing on the porch and joined Mom in the ambulance.

"You're bleeding." Drunk Mom pointed out.

Looking down at my arm, dark red blood streamed downward toward my wrist. "Looks like it."

"That little bitch," she slurred.

I shook my head, pretending like everything was fine. "She's just a confused girl, Mom. She just needs help," I lied. She would get help all right. "Are you doing okay?"

Closing her eyes, her head lolled from one side to the other. "Hungry, man."

I chuckled and leaned back against the wall in the back of the ambulance. "Me too." My hollow rumbled.

A man with skin the color and gleam of a See's chocolate bar climbed into the back of the ambulance with us as an unseen driver started the engine. It rumbled to life, and the wall against my back trembled.

"Are you going to help her or not?" Mom asked the paramedic.

"Ma'am?" he asked politely.

"Well, she's bleeding, don't you see?" She pointed a weak finger at my arm.

Rolling my eyes, I held my arm out to the man who motioned for it. "That's a deep cut, Miss. We'll need to get that bleeding under wraps first. Just sit there." He turned away from me and dug through the tiny cabinet I couldn't believe contained major life-saving devices.

Gauze and tape at the ready, the man slipped his hands into a pair of latex gloves. With precision, his slender fingers went to work bandaging my arm. His eyes slid over my evil ink every few seconds. "Interesting tattoo." He nodded toward it. "Almost lost it with this cut here." He eyed the gash that extended a few inches from the bend in my arm.

"Yeah," I said absently. "Too bad." I hadn't thought of it before, but I wondered if there was something in the tattoo itself that held power over me and my beasty.

"Drunken mistake?" He smiled a bright white grin.

Closing my eyes, I went back to leaning against the rumbling wall. "Something like that."

"Well," he said with finality as he stuck the last piece of tape to my arm. "This will help with the bleeding, but I wouldn't be surprised if you need at least a few dozen stitches."

"Thanks."

Mom snored from her spot on the gurney. The man chuckled to himself and went about checking her vitals. She'd be fine. The cut on her neck wouldn't even need stitches probably, and she'd sleep everything else off. A little therapy might be in order, but I was betting her drunken state cushioned that shock significantly.

My arm stung. Red spots seeped through the gauze in the spaces around the tape. Beneath the gauze, the tattoo, my beacon calling the beasty home, thrived. I considered slicing the thing from my flesh and ridding myself of my dark hollow for good. Knowing my luck, the bastard would love the attention and squat inside me for all eternity waiting for more.

Tattoo removal added to the list as a last resort; the original plan still stood. The only difference being I'd have to collect Angie myself. Luckily for me, I knew right where she'd be. All I needed was Mike to ensure she wasn't locked up for the weekend waiting on arraignment. Otherwise I'd be forced to strangle the little bitch in the middle of county lockup. That wouldn't do at all.

Today on People's Court.

THIRTEEN

THE COLD, STERILE HOSPITAL BROUGHT A CHILL TO MY SPINE. Arriving in an ambulance bought us a fast pass to the ER, bypassing the waiting room entirely. Mom was wheeled back into a room to be treated for shock while I was ushered to another large space lined with beds and drawn curtains where I would wait to be sewn back together.

A woman in the bed next to mine cried in pain from whatever ailment she'd come in with. Her splotchy red face and bloodshot eyes made me wonder if she was a dope sick junkie jonesing for a fix. In that case, the hospital would give her a fancy dose of methadone and send her packing until the next time she couldn't score a fix. American health care at its finest.

Here's your Band-Aid. That will be $4,000.

"Excuse me," I called out to a passing nurse. She didn't stop. Didn't even look in my direction as she hustled by. "Fuck," I whispered holding my arm.

It felt weird. Itchy and searing. The blood had stopped seeping from what I could tell, but that didn't mean I could sit there for another hour waiting to be stitched up. I had places to go and people to kidnap.

Another nurse shuffled past the large opening in the bed space where I was stuck. "Sir," I called to him. "Please stop for just a second," I pleaded with him without moving from my bed. Like the woman, he didn't stop either. I was positive they heard bitchy patients all day long begging to be seen. All I wanted was to get the fuck out of there. In fact, if I knew for certain I'd heal with a functioning arm, I'd have gotten up and walked out without looking back.

Fifteen noisy minutes passed, and no one had given me the time of day. The woman beside me hadn't shut up in the near hour I'd been there. Her screams grated on my already raw nerves and made me feel like killing things. The possibility of that was far too great to ignore, so I spent a few minutes focusing on my own pain, quelling the wicked beast inside.

At the very least I was grateful I had become aware of my possession. That was more than I could say for most people. Well, people on television anyway. The reality of the occult had already proven itself far removed from its fictional counterpart.

Sounds of heaving and the stench of vomit hurled me back into reality and away from my pain. The howling woman wretched beside me, splattering puke on the floor. Her curtain was opened enough to get a full view of her losing her cookies on the linoleum beside her bed.

"You have got to be fucking kidding me," I bellowed,

growling with frustration.

Huffing and wiping away her sloppy mouth, the woman sneered at me. “Fuck you. You don’t know what this is like.” She huffed shallow breaths as she trembled. “The need.” She raked her fingers down her face. “This is hell.”

I laughed. Full and from my belly. Slinking off the edge of the bed, I slid toward her. The mess of stomach acid and unrecognizable food lay in a puddle next to her bed.

“Hell?” I leaned in close, pulling in the stench of her puke with my nostrils. “You think you know hell?” My eyes closed, and I caroused in the smell of wretched vomit and sweat. “I am hell, *peaches*.” My deep voice garbled again and sounded like I was talking into a bowl of Jell-O. The woman’s horrified, bloodshot eyes locked onto mine. “I am sin,” I said unwillingly. “I am the rage that boils up inside you.” My nose touched the tip of hers. Sour bile filled my senses; I tasted its bitter tang on my tongue. “Your filthy soul calls to me.” I closed my eyes and smelled her skin. My wet tongue moved slowly, lapping up salty sweat from her cheek. Lips pressed to her face, I whispered, “I could wreak havoc inside your body before the sun rose in the morning.” The woman shuddered. Her screaming had stopped as she lay frozen with fear. Standing up straight, I looked down to meet the woman’s eyes. “But you’re a filthy drug-riddled whore. So shut the fuck up before you see my dark side.” I smiled. “’Kay?”

The woman didn’t respond. Her mouth, shiny with saliva and vomit, shuddered but refused to form words. Whatever pain she felt had been tramped out by fear. The hollow smiled contently inside me. I smiled too. I felt no guilt. I felt no pain. The deep darkness made sure of it. I felt invincible without reproach.

Tersely, I slid the woman's curtain shut and flopped on my bed. No one had even noticed I'd gotten up. Nurses continued to hustle by, and I hadn't seen a doctor in an hour. Mom was off in a room somewhere, and Mike was probably still back at the house sorting things out.

I picked up the phone on the wall by the bed, pressed nine, and dialed his number. "What?" He sounded panicked.

"Where is she?" I asked without any further information or cordial greeting.

He sighed. "She's with me."

Excellent. "Bring her to me."

"What?" he said quickly. "I can't do that. She has to be processed first. You're lucky she's in my car and not a squad car. She's terrified and yapping up a storm." *Fuck.* "You've been keeping a lot from me."

Fuck, fuck, fuck. "Would you rather I told you everything and put your innocent little soul in jeopardy?" My tone came out more condescending than I'd anticipated.

"Yes. Yes, I would. The truth would be appreciated."

"Fine. You want it all, you got it all." I let out a long breath and poised myself for the truth. "I just licked the sweat off a junkie and threatened to destroy her from the inside out if she didn't shut the fuck up. And I liked it." He was quiet. "I'm holding on to my sanity by a thread here, babe, and I don't know how much longer I can hang on. That woman in your car is the only thing that can stop this. You can either meet me at Sween or say goodbye now because the only other answer I have to stop this you don't want to hear."

There was a long, silent pause until I thought he'd hung up. "Do you love me?"

My hollow laughed, but my soul screamed yes. "More than

you'll ever know," I said before the darkness told me not to. Not dissimilar to the inner asshole I'd always had.

Another long pause. "If this doesn't work? If she can't fix you?"

"I destroy you all," my garbled voice said.

"Be out front in ten minutes."

I hung up without another word for fear I'd say something horrendous I couldn't take back. My arm itched, but the bleeding had stopped. I pulled the tape off and unwound the bandage from my arm. The bloody gauze fell to the floor landing in a sloppy mess I didn't bother cleaning up. An inch away from my evil ink, the long gash had become a fleshy pink scar. In the matter of an hour, a wound that the paramedic thought would need a few dozen stitches had become an annoying healing patch of new skin. My dark passenger, as Dexter would call it, had come equipped with a few superpowers. There was more happening with me than a loss of ambition and the need to feed my inner demon with the seven deadliest. I was transitioning from hell, and the side effects were awesome.

Ten minutes would be a long wait for someone to fetch me from the hospital. I wasn't about to spend one more second of it in the sick bay. "Fuck this," I murmured, and slid the curtain back.

"Miss," a nurse called to me from behind a long desk near the front door. "Where do you think you're going?"

I turned, feeling a little like Robert De Niro. *You talking to me?* "Going to find your mother," I said with a smirk. "She still dancing down at Le Pussy Cat?" The woman's face contorted and I sniggered. "You didn't give a fuck about me ten minutes ago. Why the fuck do you care now?" Her eyes went wide, but she didn't respond. "You might want to check on the junkie in bed five. She puked on the floor." I walked toward the sliding glass doors. "Deuces." I held my two fingers in the air as I sauntered out into the night.

Cold November air hit me when the glass doors slid open. At least the hospital was warmer. Surprisingly. I waited impatiently on a metal bench out front dedicated to the Johnson family, whoever the fuck they were. The metal froze my butt cheeks, my once smooth bare legs grew hair twice over with each chill. Watching for Mike's SUV, I tapped my foot against the concrete. I'd bummed a smoke off a passerby and clenched it between my fingers as it smoldered. Smoking had taken a backseat when the occult hit me hard, but it seemed the need had taken hold once again. I figured it was my last stronghold on my old life. Since sex and food were his drug of choice, it was the one vice I could cling to without fueling my hollow.

Seemingly from nowhere, a shiny black sports car screeched through the parking lot and caught my attention. It fishtailed through the winding paths between cars. Smoke billowed from the tires a few times as it squealed around sharp curves. Sliding against the curb with professional precision, the car came to a stop just a few feet in front of me and the Johnson's bench.

The passenger door flung open and a man wearing only a tank top and jeans leapt out. His milk chocolate brown hair flopped effortlessly around his face. "Dylan," Cyrus said, his chest heaving with lost breath. "Get in."

"What the fuck…? What are you…? Who is…?" I asked a million half-questions under my breath.

"Mike is meeting us at Sween. Get in. Now." He pulled me by the arm toward the car.

I puffed a few last drags off my cigarette before tossing it in the gutter. "How the fuck did you get here so fast?" I slid into the backseat.

“Magic,” Dominika answered from the driver’s seat. “Buckle up, babe.”

She slid the shifter into drive and punched it while Cyrus closed his door. Nervously, Cyrus raked his hand through his hair which upon closer inspection seemed wet. His wife beater and jeans told me Mike’s frantic phone call had interrupted him in the shower.

Meow.

“You could have skipped the clothes and gotten here in eight minutes instead,” I said seductively from the backseat.

Dominika chortled. “Are you certain we have to fix this? I like her much better this way.”

“Just drive,” he said. “Dylan, honey, when did you eat last?”

Food? “I don’t remember. Lunch I guess.”

“Stop here.” He pointed at a well-lit strip mall packed with fast food options.

“What do you suggest I order?” Dominika asked with contention.

“Bacon,” Cyrus and I said in unison.

Pork is good.

FOURTEEN

GREASE DRIPPED DOWN MY CHIN. MELTED CHEESE CLUNG TO the tips of my fingers. My stomach rumbled with satisfaction. Food had quelled the beast many times in the past but never for long. And each hour that passed, it seemed to grow stronger and more resistant to the intoxicating allure of bacon. If things didn't ease up, I would be forced to take more desperate measures.

The backseat wreaked of greasy beef and bacon. Leaning my head back against the headrest, I breathed it in. Dominika had warned me multiple times to not spill anything in her car, so I made sure to slurp down every last morsel without dropping anything. The last thing I needed was to piss off that nutbag. Although, the beasty that lurked in my hollow was curious to see who would take that fight.

The weeping willow trees draped long leafy branches over the driveway to Sween. Not necessarily indigenous to southern California, I wondered on whose authority they were planted and when. The lamplights I remembered from my first visit sat unlit. Only the moon full in the sky provided any light as we sped up the dirt and gravel road that led to the out-of-place house hidden away in Placerita Canyon.

The white antebellum loomed three-stories high, eerily encased in shadows. Not even the tiniest light shone through one of the many windows. The whiteboard porch was nearly black where no moonlight could penetrate. I'd half assumed Mike's SUV would be parked in front of the house when we pulled up. Only my shitty little Geo Metro sat, covered in bird shit and fallen branches. I thought for a moment about Tatum's car. It had been left in the parking lot at LAX, so it surely sat in police impound. I wouldn't keep her house, too many memories, but the car was nearly a necessity.

Cyrus helped me out of the slim two-door backseat of Dominika's tiny sports car. The short skirt of my little black dress slid up over my big ass as I slipped through the slender space, flashing my black panties to the world. I hadn't bothered with nylons or Spanxes. There really wasn't any point. I had been attending a funeral, who was I there to impress?

"Way too fat for this shit," I grumbled under my breath.

Cyrus held my arm as he fixed the skirt to cover my butt up again. His warm hands slid over the underside of my butt cheeks and shot an electrifying chill up my spine. Bacon and beef hadn't been enough to curb the beast. Sooner rather than later he would rear his head, and he was a pervert.

My sneakers thudded against the steps and echoed under the hollow porch. Dominika silently moved in behind me on pointed stilettos.

"Could you make any more noise?" she snapped from over my shoulder. "Like bull. Tromp, tromp, tromp." She stomped her feet through the doorway with her arms spread wide at the elbows, echoing through the house.

"Not all of us are graceful little cunts like you." I smiled sweetly and made my way to the sitting room where I would plop my ass down.

Bare knees pressed together, I did my best to feign modesty, but all the while inside I was burning with the need to screw or slaughter. Cyrus had made it clear he wasn't going down that road with me in the state I was in. Mike would do it if I made the moves, but I had to play it right, or he'd catch wind and run like last time. Dominika wasn't out of the question, but I'd save her for a very last resort. When it came down to destroying those I loved or bumping uglies with a chick, Dominika was a wise choice of lovers.

"Talk to me," Cyrus said calmly, sitting down on the blue velvet couch next to me.

I turned my head slowly. Eyes moving to look toward him first. "About what?" A coy smile turned the corners of my mouth upward.

Never in my life had I been so consumed by a need I couldn't pin down. My human brain told me food, sex, even blood would curb my appetite, but still, the hollow grew. The apathetic hollow, the fiery rage, the burning desire to fuck something or eat something, had manifested itself as human wants, but it was so much simpler than that. The answer had been right there all along. I'd said it myself. I am sin.

No pork product, no dicking, not even wrathful decimation would satiate the beast. He—or she, there was no clear distinction—would fester and boil in my soul until it too turned black, until the evil took over and Dylan Hart was finally the monster she was destined to become.

"*The Sound of Music*," he said blankly.

"Swiss Alps, my favorite things, Julie Andrew's *Sound of Music*?" He nodded, his hair soft and wavy around his face. "Why the fuck would I talk about that?"

He leaned back away from me. "Because it's the most wholesome subject I can imagine."

"Have you ever seen it?" I doubted quite seriously he had and decided if I was wrong, he was far gayer than he'd let on.

"Perhaps once. Julie Andrews is a vision in a habit."

I shook my head. "I'll gladly talk about secret romance, sexual tension, and the threat of war." Smiling, I realized he was doing his best to remain as far from me as possible. "Why are you all the way over there?"

He chuckled nervously. "Because it's best for both of us."

"What's up your ass, chicken?" I jutted my chin in his direction.

His Adam's apple bobbed when he swallowed hard. Standing, he shoved his hands in his pockets. "You know why." Curved muscles on his shoulders contracted slowly as he dug around in his pockets with a nervousness I'd never seen him possess. "I brought you something… odd. Mike said it might help." From his pocket, he produced a tightly wrapped white joint.

My eyes went wide, and I smiled. I nearly licked my chops at the sight but decided against it. The eternal dark hollow had grown strong and fierce, but I refused to let myself go completely. Every day in the last week when I'd smoked weed, the beast left me be for a while. I didn't want to know why, though my deep curiosity burned to know, all I cared about was the fact that it worked. Almost better than bacon.

I stood and snatched my temporary cure from between his pinched fingers. "Yoink," I offered, holding it up to him. "Join me?"

"No, thank you." He looked away from me. "And if you don't mind, please smoke that upstairs. Your room is as you left it."

"My room?" I hadn't realized I was a permanent resident.

"Your dead space," Dominika clarified from the stairs. It was an *interesting* way to put it, and I stood in the middle of the room staring at her. "Are we going to kill that joint or are you just going to stand there staring at me?"

Dominika the pothead, hadn't seen that coming. Although she did strike me as a woman of many vices and not one ounce of conscience in the matter. If I wasn't careful, I'd be just like her. Rotten.

I bound up the stairs with an energy I'd been lacking for months. There was no way Dominika and I would ever be pals, but in a weird way, I trusted her more than the men in my life. She was the only one who didn't feel the need to lie to me. And Genevieve. Maybe it was just a woman thing.

In the room, Dominika opened a small drawer in a jewelry box on the vanity. She pulled out a lighter and a quarter-sized cone of incense. She placed the cone on a saucer decorated with some sort of fancy design and lit the tip. It smoldered a moment before the top turned orange and puffs of smoke undulated from it.

I sat crisscross on the bed, joint in hand. The sticky bud gloriously pungent through the thin white paper. I hadn't bothered asking where he'd gotten an expertly rolled joint in a matter of ten minutes. A man like Cyrus Atossa could probably score anything in ten minutes.

You want a toe? I can get you a toe.

"What is it about this do you think helps me and my beasty?" Mumbled and rushed, my words mashed together in more of a growl than actual speech.

"Your beasty?" Dominika questioned, sitting gently on the edge of the bed. "Curious way to put it." Slender, pale shoulders shrugged delicately. "Perhaps it pulls you away from your body and into a plane of existence more attune with the earth." She plucked the unlit joint from my fingers. "Or perhaps your beasty simply enjoys the taste of it."

Lighting the pinched end of the joint, Dominika puffed at it until it lit and turned orange like the incense had. Smoke billowed out the other end filling the room with the smell of pot. My mother would have been banging down the door by that point, if she hadn't been sitting in a hospital bed. I was certain Mike ensured an overnight stay for her before he sped off into the night after me. She'd be safe until I could get my shit together and nix the beasty for good.

I puffed out smoke rings as the drug began to take hold. "My compliments to the chef." I laughed and passed it back to her.

The pot was top shelf and took effect in no time. My heavy lids slowly blinked closed. Open. Closed again. "Too bad I didn't have this shit a few nights ago. I might not have torn a hole into Mike's shoulder." Tangy blood memories took me back to that night and simultaneously, I shivered and grinned.

Dominika held the joint delicately between her fingers and pulled a long drag. "Darling, your need to devour is in its infancy. That boy would have been consumed in more ways than one had your so-called beasty been unleashed." She ran a tongue over her lips as she blew out smoke, her blue eyes mostly closed. "The sinful thing inside you tickles at the fantasies you already have. Making you ache to fulfill them." She handed me the joint and leaned in close. "You could be ferocious if given the opportunity." She tapped a single, slender finger down my cheek. "All. By. Your. Lonesome."

Joint clenched between my chubby fingers, I raised a skeptical brow at her. "It's coming soon, and I fear I won't be able to stop it."

Shaking her head, she leaned back against the bedpost at the foot. "Fear what you must. There is nothing wrong with a woman who takes what she wants."

I leaned back too, pinching the dying joint in my fingers. "What I want will hurt people I care about."

She closed her eyes and chuckled lightly. "There is your problem. To be truly ruthless is to be eternally alone." She let out a long sigh. "Should your fears prove correct, you will be forced to make a choice. Kill those you love. Or kill yourself." She pulled her long legs up on the bed, laying them over mine. "My money is on your beasty."

Her bare legs touched mine as she moved them tickling along the naked flesh. "I think you underestimate me."

"Perhaps." She shrugged. "I can smell the hell that clings to you." She licked her lips. "It smells of sex and rage." A smile spread across her face. "What do you have hidden inside that head of yours, dirty girl?"

Mostly sex and rage. "More than I'd like to admit."

"Should you change your mind, I'm open to the opportunity to see this savage little beast inside."

"Why am I so interesting? Don't Cyrus and the fang gang keep you entertained?"

"Boring." She stretched the word out as long as humanly possible. Or inhumanly. "At least Malcolm had some balls. Cyrus, ugh." She rolled her eyes.

"He's not really cut out for this Primus gig."

"Nicolas should have known better."

"So, what, this guy Nicolas just said, hey, Cyrus, you're the new Primus if I die? I mean, aren't there rules?"

"Rules?" She tipped her head side to side. "In politics, there are no rules, but yes, the community adheres to rules, as you call them." She crawled on hands and knees to lay beside me. "In love? There are no boundaries."

"Tell me about it." I thought of Mike.

"Malcolm didn't follow the rules. Killing Nicolas bought him his seat as Primus, but House of Sandorus had very specific instructions should Nicolas die. Sher, Cyrus, was to take his seat as Primus."

"Shouldn't you have been Primus? I mean, weren't you and Nicolas hanging together before Cyrus came along?"

She let out a long quiet sigh. "Technically, yes, but once Cyrus became immortal that changed. Nicolas practically worshipped the little shit. Cyrus was seated as Secondus, and I was demoted to Chancellor."

"So why didn't Malcolm just appoint new staff and nix you and Cyrus?"

I felt her shrug beside me without having to look at her. "I was of no consequence in his mind. And Cyrus… was an asset. One of a kind. Malcolm knew he would come in handy someday. Cyrus never stood against him, always followed commands. Waiting for his time to take his rightful seat. Over the last few decades, I thought many times of killing him myself."

"Why didn't you?"

She shook her head, jiggling the bed. "Regina?"

"Yeah."

"Yeah."

I thought on that for a minute. "So it's true? These headless girls are executed vamps?"

"Yes, of course."

"Man, Reggie? I didn't think she was… the real deal." I recalled the moments I'd spent with her and the stories I'd heard about her life in Fresno. "She was like you?"

"Yes, of course. Well, not like *me*. She still had many, many years to lose herself. Malcolm had become intrigued by her and sent Cyrus to fetch her like a puppy dog. It didn't take long before he cast her aside to sling beers to the sweaty masses."

"And Azelie and Marienne had her in their clutches."

She jiggled the bed again. "And she lost her head. Steep

price to pay for eternal youth."

"Tell that to the Botox bitches in Beverly Hills."

"Sadly, that lovely quip was wasted on the likes of Regina Laurant." Dominika's flat tone sent chills down my spine.

Intuition took over, drawing from my depths the knowledge that Dominika had been the one to pull the trigger on Reggie, so to speak. Whether Malcolm had ordered it or she'd taken it upon herself, Dominika had a black mark on her soul and my beast could smell it. I turned my head slowly to see her expression and met her nose to nose. Stark blue eyes burrowed into mine. A sinister grin spread across her face.

"Where is that little beasty hiding?" she whispered against my lips. Her eyes slid over me, searching my own eyes for the hollow I'd repressed with primo weed. "Tsk, tsk, tsk," she clucked her tongue, "you can't hide from me." My heart pounded as her breath fell softly over my mouth. "Come out, come out, wherever you are." Her sultry voice tickled over my skin, drawing goosebumps to the surface.

My insides rumbled. "I'd really appreciate if you didn't taunt the devil in me," I whispered back.

"Finding it hard to hold in?"

"Yes." The word slid out in a garbled hiss. I swallowed it back. "Why did you kill Regina?" I pushed the words through my lips.

She let out a loud burst of a laugh. "That stupid girl practically killed herself. Like all those other idiots. Think they know what they're doing." Her eyes moved over me. "Just like some other stupid girl I know."

Long, rumbling sounds reverberated through my chest.

"Fuck you," I garbled.

"There you are, sexy, bad beasty. Give us a kiss?" She laughed and pressed her lips to mine.

The dark hollow inside responded instantly and thundered to life. More than Cyrus. More than Mike. Dominika taunted the sinful thing, she'd called it out, and we wanted her. So, so bad. My arms clamped around her body and pulled her in tight. She squealed, provoking the beast further. A growl rumbled up my throat. Her hands slid up my bare thighs, squeezing the soft cushion of my ass, nails digging into my cheeks. I plunged my tongue into her mouth, forcing her mouth open wide.

Hands groping. Legs intertwined. Jolts of unadulterated passion shocked my naughty bits. Sounds of pleasure rolled up Dominika's throat and against my lips. One hand wrapped around the back of her head, I used the other to slide the slit in her dress, exposing the long pale expanse of her thigh. I gripped it with immovable strength. Supple in my grasp, soft skin beckoned us like a fluffy white rabbit to a hungry fox. My fingers played over the soft skin as she fought against me. I squeezed, digging my nails into her; claws against flesh. Her squeal taunted us. I dug deeper, pressing myself against her lean body, taking what I wanted. Devouring her in every way.

Her eyes flew open and met mine. Wild and fierce, my eyes burrowed into hers while we kissed. Fear slid over the beautiful cobalt eyes I stared into. She pushed against me, but I refused to budge. She wanted a kiss—I was giving her one. She tempted the beast and got the horns.

Screams came from deep in her throat. Blood tempted my tongue. I hadn't intended it, but somehow she was bleeding.

The beast flailed within me. I wanted her. I craved her screams in my bones. The taste of her blood on my tongue only furthered the advances of the beast she'd lured to the surface. The line between my beast and I blurred with sex and death. I shoved my hand up her dress, finding a bare ass I could already feel between my teeth. Death grip on her plump cheek, I pulled her body against mine. She clawed at me with frantic flailing hands. My long, wet tongue licked her clenched lips. Fear dripped from her skin; centuries old and intoxicating. Drunk with passion, I buried my face in her boobs, in search of purchase. We'd sink our teeth in and eat her from the top down. We wanted to suck the marrow from her bones while she writhed in agony.

Overpowering me with preternatural strength, she rolled me over onto my back, straddling me. A grin spread across my face, and I pressed myself into her. The ripping sound of her dress came a moment before her fist crunched against the side of my face. Released from my grasp, she sat up straight. Blood tinged her bottom lip red.

The door flung open wide and slammed against the wall. "What is happening here?" Cyrus bellowed.

Dominika's eyes met mine, panicked. She'd done it to herself. Every last drop of it.

"On any other occasion, I would not hesitate having a seat and allowing this to continue, but your detective has just pulled up out front."

My detective? "Mike! Fuck." Self-preservation won the battle between beast and host. I pushed her off me, and she went easily. Sitting up, I fixed my hair and pulled my skirt down over my stomach.

Dominika sat huddled on the bed. The slit in her dress had ripped to her hip. Her lean thigh exposed, my fingers reached out unwillingly and tickled down the length of it to her knee.

"Well, this *is* an interesting development." Cyrus ran his hand through his hair.

"Stop it." Dominika flipped my hand off her leg.

Leaning close to her face, I whispered. "Don't entice me again. I'm doing well not killing things I actually *like*. Lord knows what will happen to *you*." Sliding off the bed, I wished I hadn't said that. The more time I spent with her, the more I realized Dominika was me, had I been granted hundreds of years to live.

What little control I'd had over my hollow place was fading fast. Dominika had torn my walls down with her bare hands and left me struggling to regain my composure. Cyrus stood at the door, hands clamped to the sides of his face. Dominika slinked off the bed and around the foot toward Cyrus. I'd never seen her speechless, but that was the only way to describe her state.

Not wanting her to storm out and rat me out to Mike, I stalled, making sure I knew where I stood with her before she walked out the door.

"Hey," I called out to her. She turned and looked at me over her shoulder. "What did you expect?" Her eyes, sad for the first time, met mine. "This isn't a game. This is my life, my soul on the line here. Did you really think something this powerful was going to take you out for a dinner and movie?"

Letting out a long, ragged breath, she looked away from me. "I expected comradery in our misery. Your beast and I."

Looking at Cyrus, she placed a hand flat against his chest. "There's no time," she whispered. I watched her lips move quickly. Her eyes slid to me and back again. "She's hollow inside." Meeting my eyes full on, she whispered to Cyrus. "Filled only by malevolence."

The front door slammed shut and raucous, clambering footsteps echoed from the hardwood up the stairs. Cyrus poked his head out the open door and down the hallway. Moving a morose Dominika out into the hall, he leaned into the room toward me.

"For all our sakes, please, please hold on." Quickly, he shuffled out of the room.

I plopped on the bed halfheartedly, tears welling in my eyes. The hollow within me had ignited with Dominika's teasing, but I was still in there too. I knew it. I had to be. Whatever squatted inside me couldn't cry. It couldn't feel the pain locked inside me. No. The beast had washed it away with the scent of Tatum. It ran from the sound of Mike but wanted so much to gobble him up that it ached deep inside me. With the help of Ms. Frizzle, I would have been witness to an all-out battle between my soul and the beasty that threatened to take it over. There wasn't time for answers. No time to run and hide. I was slipping away.

The half-smoked joint sat on the foot of the bed with the lighter Dominika left there. Quickly, I sparked it up and pulled long, deep drags into my lungs. Smoke billowed from between my lips when Mike barreled through the doorway.

"Now? You're doing that now?" he questioned, shutting the door behind him. "Now is definitely not the time for that." He pointed at my drugs. "You've got to come down—"

“You gave it to me,” I exclaimed.

“Yes, but—”

“It’s the only thing standing between me and the thing that’s threatening to rip me from this world for good,” I proclaimed during a minute space of lucidity.

“What?” He walked closer to me, close enough to touch.

I shook my head and stamped out the glowing cherry against the side of the lighter. “There’s something inside of me that wants desperately to take me over. I don’t know what it wants, but I know I’m fueling it with my sins.” I sounded deranged even to myself.

He squatted down in front of me. “Babe, what are you talking about?” His voice was calm and reassuring, as if he didn’t believe me.

“You know. I know you do.” I forced him to see me for what I was. I begged him with my eyes to look deep and see the thing slithering around in there. “I brought something back with me, and now it’s squatting inside, taking over my soul.” Fear crept up my throat and quivered in my voice.

“What’s inside of you?” His brows turned up in the center as sadness took hold of him. It wasn’t the look of fear I’d expected. It was the look of pity.

Leaning in close enough to whisper the word I’d refused to say for days, even in my own head, I said, “The devil.” My words slid over his skin, drawing out a shiver.

Goosebumps sprang up along the tender skin of his neck. I caught sight of the reaction, and my hunger became giddy with delight. The scent of his skin drew me closer to him. I recalled the taste of his blood in my mouth and licked my lips to drag the memory out further. Closing my eyes, I pulled the lobe of his ear into my mouth with my tongue. A heavy sigh escaped his lips. Running my tongue over the soft skin, I slid off the edge of the bed to straddle his lap, pushing him to his knees.

"Dylan," he said softly. "The devil isn't real."

A delicate snigger rumbled in my throat. "Many things are real, my love. You only have to open your eyes and look."

He moved his head away from me, a love-drunk smile spread across his face. His eyes met mine. In an instant, his hands were on my hips moving me away from him. He scrambled to his feet and stood, leaving me sitting on the floor.

"What the fuck was that?" he yelled, pointing at me and hysterically running his hands through his hair. "Babe, what the fuck was that?"

I sat on the floor laughing. Gurgling as though I was laughing into a bowl of Jell-O again.

The door flung open behind him as the familiar *thunk* of a wooden leg clicked into the room. "The devil, boy. Don't you listen?" Lupe stood in the doorway, the smoldering stump of a cigar bobbed in her lips as she spoke.

"Actually," a tiny, familiar voice spoke up from behind her, "it's not the devil. It's probably Ashmedai." Angie's petite frame moved in behind Lupe. "He's not the devil...." Her unsure voice trailed off.

My jaw dropped to the floor. Lupe and Angie in one room. I didn't know how it happened, but they couldn't have come at a better time. Mike was about to be gobbled up whole.

Looking back and forth between the two I quickly wondered if the other knew who they were standing beside. I hoped they never figured it out. Though a part of me, the part the hollow had swallowed up and kept for himself, couldn't wait to watch when they did.

Battle royale. May the best bitch win. Or witch. Whatever.

FIFTEEN

"HOW?" I POINTED AT LUPE FROM MY SPOT ON THE FLOOR. My laughter had ceased the moment Angie walked in the door. Like it had with Mike, the beasty scurried away and hid at the sound of her voice.

Lupe shot Mike an exasperated look. "Idle threats."

Mike, still stunned at my impromptu revelation, didn't have time to sugarcoat things. "I pointed a gun at her until she got into my car."

"That is… kinda sexy," I said, still sitting on the floor. "And really quite smart." I didn't know what to say. He'd risked his career, his life, for me. "Thank you."

"Don't mention it," he mumbled and moved away from me. Whatever he was thinking, the fear he'd had of me was back. "Can we get started figuring out how to solve this?" His eyes said more than his words and I worried he'd turn tail and run. It was one thing to say you're okay with something, it was totally different when it came right down to doing it.

"I have to agree," I said. "Lucidity doesn't seem to be my strong suit at the moment." *Thanks a fucking lot, Dominika.* "Also, the longer we sit here, the more I'll want to rip your hearts out through your chest cavity. Just saying," I added, looking away from the terrified eyes glaring at me.

"Right," Lupe said, planting her hands on her hips. "Although I do recall refusing to help you," she glared at Mike, "it seems I have no choice." She clucked her tongue, looking around the room. "Who's smoking the marijuanas?" She added an s at the end, and it made me laugh.

"Seems to be the only thing that keeps whatever this is at bay." My brain was foggy, but I was me again. For the time being. "That and food." She scrunched her brows at me. "Well, meat." Her head lowered, and she looked at me from under her brow. "Bacon. It's mostly bacon."

"And sex," Mike piped in. "She's generally cantankerous." *Quite the word choice*. "Since she came back…" He slowed his pace and looked at Angie, not knowing fully who she was. "…from vacation… she's been… frisky."

That was an understatement.

"Well," Angie guffawed, "yeah, that's what Ashmedai is good for."

Everyone turned to look at the little blonde girl. No one but she and I knew why she was important, or what she'd done to me. Or more importantly in Lupe's case, why she'd done it.

"What'd you say, girl?" Lupe turned slowly to look over her shoulder at Angie.

Angie shimmied her way around Lupe and into the room

and stood between Mike and me. "Ashmedai." Her nonchalant attitude made me want to punch her in the throat. She walked toward me and held my arm up. "See?" She asked of my evil ink. "His mark." Dropping my arm, she stood up straight and shrugged. "I'm only assuming here, but I don't see any other option. Unless, of course, she pissed off someone else and they summoned some other demon as retribution." She laughed. "But that would just be weird. Right?" She looked around at our shocked faces. "I mean, who's that unlucky to be cursed twice?" When no one spoke or even moved, her face fell. "Right?"

"You're obviously new here," Mike said, moving away from her and toward the door. Away from me.

Rubbing my hand over my forehead, I clarified. "You are not the first… curse I've had." I stopped and lifted my hefty body off the floor to stand. "In fact, the line between this," I held up my arm, "and that is nearly nonexistent at this point."

"Well, shit." She shook her head and looked at Lupe. "I don't know how this happened." She held a hand out to me. "Possession is rare, and that wasn't what he was sent here for in the first place. Someone would have to be wide open to let him in." She held her arms out wide.

My eyes shot to Lupe. I squinted them angrily at her. "I *was* wide open," I said through gritted teeth.

"Oh." Her tiny mouth made a perfect O as she raised two blonde eyebrows. "Then I don't know how to help you."

"What?" I stomped toward her. "You were my only hope. My fucking Obi-Wan. You better figure it the fuck out and quick because my resolve is fading fast and you're at the top of my shit list."

Her hands shook, and she shoved them into her pockets.

"Okay, okay," she said softly. "Um," she looked back at Lupe, "we can try to draw him out."

"Like an exorcism?" Mike asked.

"Kind of, yeah." Angie nodded. Lupe hadn't said a word.

"So you're saying she's possessed… by the devil?" His tone said he wasn't buying it.

Angie rolled her eyes dramatically, reminding me of her age. "Not exactly. God and Devil are too simple for what you're dealing with. The actual matters of the universe are more complex than that."

"Like vampires, and voodoo, and curses, and demons?" I'd really thought his skepticism was out the window.

"Sure." Angie nodded. "I don't have any supplies with me. But I think she brought some along just in case." She thumbed Lupe. "We can get set up in here and… yeah." She nodded enthusiastically.

I squinted my eyes suspiciously at her. The upbeat attitude she had was unnerving for the situation. The fact that Lupe hadn't moved a muscle in the time Angie had the floor bothered me. Angie had been a vampire wannabe the first time I'd met her. Five months later and she was cracked out on Meth, hanging with black magic folks, summoning demons to hunt me down. Her street cred was lacking, to say the least.

"Good. Hurry it up." Mike nodded in her direction, and she scuttled out the door. Lupe didn't budge, her eyes burrowed into me. "How much of that am I expected to believe?" he asked Lupe.

Honey brown eyes searched my face a second before moving to look at him. "All of it." She turned on her heel and thudded down the hall.

Mike melodramatically turned to look at me. Fear still had

a stronghold on him. He seemed to trust Lupe more than the tweaker, or me for that matter, and the idea left him terrified.

Not wanting to face his scrutiny, I made up an excuse to get me out of the room. "I have to pee." Refusing to meet his eyes, I scurried past him and out the door.

I felt his hand graze my arm as I passed but I ignored it. In reality, I knew he didn't really want to touch me. He'd seen something in me, something malicious. His literal thinking, rational brain surely interpreted whatever he saw as something I'd done. Something I'd made up. Like the demon inside me. I closed the bathroom door and hoped Lupe could reason with him.

Someone had replaced the broken bulb overhead. I'd have laid down money they had a housekeeper of some sort keeping up on the place. Cold water splashed over my face. My eyes closed, I let the sensation wash over me. The water cooled my skin immediately. I leaned over the sink on my elbows as drips fell from the tip of my nose into the basin. Mike's terrified image flashed in my head. He couldn't fear me now. I needed him. I needed his head in the game. He'd risked everything to bring me what, *who*, I needed to get better. What I needed most was him, and I was losing him every chance I got. That fucking thing inside me hated Mike for whatever reason and seemed to want him gone more than anyone. That alone made him my strongest ally.

Lifting my head from the sink, I met my own eyes in the mirror. Gaunt, drawn cheeks and darkened rims around my eyes stared back. I looked as dead as I felt inside. Green eyes glistened and shimmered, a sudden shift to blue. "What the fuck?" I leaned closer to the mirror and watched with wide eyes as my reflection morphed into the face of my dead best friend.

"He thinks you've really lost it," she said in my voice. Blonde hair clung to her forehead where the water had stuck to it.

"I'm talking to my dead best friend in the mirror. I think I lost it a long time ago." I talked, but her mouth moved too.

"He's going to lock you up in the nut house."

"I know."

"You can't let him."

"Stop talking to me and he won't."

"Dylan, you know better than to actually think it's me doing the talking." She smiled. We leaned closer to each other and spoke in a whisper. "He thinks you're a nutbag and he is going to lock you away from the world." We shook our head. "We can't have that."

"Then what the hell am I supposed to do?" I asked, hoping for something prolific.

"Fake it."

"That's all? What if he doesn't believe?"

"Make him believe." She placed a hand on the mirror. Her pink palm marred with the mark of Ashmedai.

I matched her action and pressed my hand to hers. Blue eyes turned green, and again I stared at myself in the mirror. As much as I wished I'd been talking to my friend, I knew better. The thing inside me was a trickster and seemed to enjoy playing with my emotions. And those of the people I loved.

My hand slid down the glass with a squeak, leaving behind an elongated smear. Mike had to believe me. The witch bitches had to figure it out and force the son of a bitch out of me. If it didn't work, if that thing didn't leave, I would be left with two options, fake it or kill them all.

BANG, BANG, BANG.

I jumped at the sound of someone fervently banging on the

bathroom door.

"It's time," Dominika snarled through the thick wood.

Regaining my composure, I looked at myself one last time. I'd done the same moments before Lupe had sent me on "vacation." I hoped this excursion had a better outcome. For the sake of everyone involved. Mike could talk a big game, but I knew whatever he had to do to handle me would destroy him in the end. If I didn't do it first.

"It's time." I winked at my own reflection. "Ashmedai," I said in the mirror. The name rolled off my tongue as though I'd been saying it for years. "You're out of here, motherfucker." I spoke at my reflection to the thing inside me.

Or I'll be taking it for a long time to come.

SIXTEEN

EVERYONE STOPPED TALKING AND LOOKED AT ME WHEN I stepped off the last step. Expressions ranged from wretched to irritated as each of them watched me walk across the room. An aura of malice surrounded me as I focused my energy on taking each step as normally as I could. The hollow wasn't far from the surface now; each step clicked and ticked in my head.

"We ready to get this show on the road?" My voice, a deep unnatural rumbling, echoed through the room. The hollow crept up inside me and tickled the back of my throat with phantom claws. Never before had I been so on the edge of darkness. Teetering on one foot, clutching to an avant-garde umbrella high above my head, as dramatic circus music played in the background. I held a smile on my face, but it was a façade for the horror happening inside me.

Fake it.

Lupe eyed Angie suspiciously from the corner of her eye. The woman may have been a selfish bitch, but she was far from ignorant. It wouldn't be long before she locked on to what her intuition was telling her. Angie was a damn bobblehead, it seemed, and it would certainly take her longer to figure out who the old lady on the wooden leg truly was. Lupe, on the other hand, had been silently processing the situation since the moment Angie started running her mouth. I didn't know what Mike had told either of them, but he didn't have the full story to blab either way.

"Before I can help you, I need to know how this came about." Lupe flicked her finger back and forth between Angie and me. "Because I am confused."

"Well," Angie took a deep breath, "it's a funny story. See, a few weeks ago Dylan shows up out of nowhere, looking for my friend Zeph." Her words were speedy, rambling.

"Zeph?" Lupe's brow raised.

"Yeah, he was my boyfriend, kind of." She breathed in sharply. "Anyway, Dylan shows up with this guy." She pointed to Cyrus who stood behind her. "And—" Stopping short she did a double take. "Who oddly enough I'd met ages ago in another life." She spoke so fast we found it hard to keep up. Her hands flailed in front of her exaggerating her words.

"Did you do a bunch of drugs or something?" I asked, looking to Mike from the corner of my eye. He dropped his head into his hands, shamefully. "You didn't? Holding an old woman at gunpoint *and* giving a suspect drugs? You're really shooting for officer of the year."

"I didn't give it to her. She had it on her. I just let her take it. You want her running to my supervisor squealing about this?"

He had a point, but if the roles were reversed, I'd have had her in my clutches without the use of illegal drugs. "I'm lucky there are more fucked-up people out there tonight to give a shit about this one." He thumbed her direction.

"Do you think she's going to be worth a shit now?"

"I'm functioning." Angie's voice was shrill. Her eyes wide, her jaw wiggled back and forth uncontrollably.

"Aye," Lupe yelled and thumped across the room to Cyrus. "This is what you dragged me into?" She flung her hand toward Angie. "Drugs and devils. I can't be a part of this. I can't. Devils are not allowed."

"Ugh," Angie sighed, "Not the *devil.* I already said that. Ashmedai."

Cyrus's eyes shot up and focused on her. "Why do you speak that name in this house?"

"Because that's his name." Her Valley Girl tone brought an annoyed look to Dominika's face.

Cyrus moved swiftly toward the girl, wrapping large hands around her spindly arms. "You summoned the seventh prince as retribution for what we did?" She nodded slowly. "Do you realize what you've done?"

"Do *you*?" I asked him, surprised he recognized the name of a demon that was taking me over.

"Yes." He closed his eyes and let her go. "Aeshma, a vile demon, ruler of moral wickedness, and devourer of wrathful sins. He is the prince of lust, among other things." Cyrus's perfect green eyes met mine. In them, despair. "Is this who has been tormenting you?"

"I'm not a professional, but I'd have to say yes." I shrugged. My hollow tingled deep inside. The possibility of that tingle being a direct response to their questioning grew as it became an itch in the back of my throat.

He let out a long shuddering breath. “This is more than I can fathom.” He looked at Angie. “How could you ever imagine unleashing Aeshma, Ashmedai, whatever he is called these days, upon the world?”

Angie shrugged. “Terry said Ashmedai would make sure she got what she deserved.”

“A shrug? That’s what we get? A shrug?” My shrill voice annoyed even me. “And how in the fuck do you know this?” I turned to ask Cyrus.

“Ashmedai has had many names in many languages. My country called him Aeshma. It is said he is the bearer of three heads. A serpent, a lion, and goat. He is fierce and unrelenting in his wrath and will use these powers to unfold all of humanity from the inside out.”

“Like he’s been doing to me for days.”

“Yes.” He grabbed Angie by her arm. “You stupid girl,” he said through gritted teeth. “Do you realize what you’ve done? Do you?” She shook her head, fear washing over her face. “We cannot undo this,” he whispered. “You have brought hell upon us.” His eyes glowed yellow-green, and a rumbling growl shook from his chest.

Mike shoved his hands in his pockets, watching as Cyrus threatened the girl with his eyes. Any other day he would have jumped in and saved the day. Hero Mike was gone. I’d swallowed him whole.

Dominika smiled a devious grin and folded her arms across her heaving chest. If I didn’t know better, I would have said the scene was turning her on. As his energy washed over the room, it tickled along my skin, bringing out goosebumps and tantalizing my hollow. Ashmedai enjoyed the rage in his voice and fed on the energy rolling off him.

"I'm sorry," Angie's tiny voice squeaked out. "I was angry. She took my Zeph, and my coven blamed me. I couldn't stop them." I doubted that was true, but didn't doubt for a second she hadn't acted alone. "I just wanted to know what happened to him." She cried.

Lupe's leg thudded against the wood floor as she stomped toward the pathetic girl. "I killed the stupid boy. He disgraced my family. My heritage." She moved her face closer to Angie's. "For you." The hate in her voice tugged at the beasty. "I should kill you now for being so stupid."

She pushed a single finger against Angie's forehead. Instantly, Angie's head lolled to the side, and she went limp. Cyrus caught her before she tumbled to the floor. Mike ripped his hands from his pockets and jolted closer.

"What in the fuck?" Mike shouted. My eyes wide, I tried to make sense of what I'd just seen.

"Hold your pants, boy. She's alive." Lupe thudded across the room to a chalk outline on the floor. "Just couldn't stand the sound of her breath."

Can you teach me that trick?

"We can't stop this," Cyrus said to Lupe, holding a hand out to me.

"Thanks for the vote of confidence." I folded my arms over my chest.

"Lies only feed the beast." *Wish I would have known that ages ago.* "Only a Yasna ritual can rid her of this affliction."

"Good. Good. Do it."

Cyrus ran his hand over his hair. "It's not that easy. Yasna is only performed by a Motilhub, a high priest. And only in a fire temple. This..." He looked slowly around the room. "...this is a house of sin." His eyes met mine. The yellow glow was gone, and his beautiful green eyes were back. "This is *his* house."

I nodded, pulling the corners of my mouth down. "Sounds about right."

"What the fuck are we supposed to do now? Huh?" Mike's hostile tone brought a scoff from Dominika.

"I'll take her." She blew me a kiss, and I caught it. Her eyes moved away from mine quickly, embarrassed I hadn't forgotten where we'd began our little tryst.

Mike's eyes squinted as he looked back and forth between us. Cyrus caught the exchange and moved away to lay Angie down on the sofa.

"Shut up," Lupe said around a freshly lit cigar. "Your demon may have a Hebrew name, but this Mexican witch is in America and in America we get shit done."

Impressed, I couldn't help but laugh. "That's the attitude I'm looking for." I looked back and forth between Mike and Cyrus while I moved closer to the woman with a plan.

"Dylan," Cyrus called after me. "Aeshma is powerful." He eyed Lupe and gripped my arms. "More powerful than you can imagine."

"Aye. Of course he is. Made himself at home in an empty vessel. Big tough guy." She bobbed her head back and forth, her salt-and-peppered auburn bun bounced on her head. "She was wide open when that little bitch summoned him." *Because of you.* "Her body lay here defenseless for days while she tried to crawl back up from his world." *Also you.* "That thing clung to her like a parasite, slithering his way into this world. It won't be long before he takes her completely. Her mind will wither and her body will die as it should have while it laid up in that bed. When she is gone, when this vessel is of no use, he will move along to the nearest empty sinner. This will happen until he has become so powerful no one can stop him." She poured salt lines on the floor. Smoke encircled her head. "Do not think for one moment I am here to help any one of you. I am here to save myself from certain damnation."

Glad you cleared that up.

"What's the plan then?" Mike asked, standing far away from me.

Lupe stopped what she was doing and eyed us all. "What has happened here?"

Everyone looked at each other, but no one spoke. Dominika watched me from beneath black lashes. Cyrus moved his eyes over her and me both. Mike's eyes burrowed into the side of my head as I refused to meet anyone's eyes.

"Dylan has not been herself, obviously," Cyrus finally answered.

Lupe gnawed on the end of her cigar, ash fell to the floor. "Humph, damnation stares you in the face, and yet your lies don't stop. When will you learn?"

The hollow rumbled deep inside me. Daring me to lie and manipulate. He was strong, his will was a worthy adversary, but Aeshma didn't know who he was fucking with. "I bit the shit out of Mike while I was trying to get into his pants. Then he forgave me. But then I can't stop hitting on people. Or eating meat. And I want blood. And I'm so mean, I can't stop. Oh, fuck, and Dominika and I totally made out upstairs." The truth all poured out in one long string of words. Mike's breath caught in his throat. "Sorry," I said, shooting him a side glance.

Nodding, she closed her eyes. "How are you feeling now?"

I stopped and focused on my hollow. "Empty." Swallowing hard, my throat ached. "And my throat hurts." Shaking my head, I moved closer to her, and she backed away. "It's weird. I don't have control over it, and sometimes there's no warning. Other times I can feel it rumbling around in there preparing to strike. Before Mike came into the room, I could have devoured Dominika and not thought twice about it." I stopped and thought. "He has a weird effect on me. His voice can send the dark beasty slithering back home to the hollow place, but in the same instant, I'm fighting away a desire for him so intense it feels like I can't breathe." Mike pulled in a sharp inhale.

She puffed on her cigar. "You and he are bound together. He holds your soul on this earth. Of all the unfortunate coincidences leading up to this moment, binding the two of you was the one good thing." Her honey eyes landed on Mike. "You are her anchor." He swallowed hard. "I know you're scared, but we have no time for that now. In the moments to come, you will be the one solid footing she has on her own soul and this world." Mike ran two hands over either side of his head, letting out a long, desperate sigh. "Man up, it's time we ended this for good." She thudded away with her salt. "I'm sick of looking at your faces," she mumbled.

"What about her?" Dominika nodded in the direction of the sleeping Angie.

Lupe grunted as she dumped salt. "She's of no use." The cigar made her words mumbled. "Unless we can kill her." She eyed Mike, who didn't say a word in response.

What was one tweaker witch bitch in the grand scheme? Right?

"Do what needs to be done." Everyone turned slowly to look at Mike. "After tonight, I'm done with this." He looked at me. "You're done with this. Whatever all of this is, we're not going to be a part of it." Back to Lupe. "And you, you're going to make damn certain this girl is free of whatever evil shit she's got on her, or you'll have bigger shit to worry about than salt and tweakers."

Lupe waved a hand at him, dismissing his threats. "Come on," she called to me, but I didn't move. "We don't have all night. I want to get this done with."

Moving hurriedly to the circle surrounded by squiggly things that somewhat matched my evil ink, I took one last look at Mike. Feeling mostly myself for the moment, I wanted to reach out to him and never let go. I begged him with my eyes to force the beast away forever so I could finally be just normal.

"I'm sorry," I said softly to Mike. "Don't leave me," I whimpered quietly. He'd said those exact words to me a long time ago. Finally, I knew the fear he felt while he watched me turn my back to him and walk away.

"Never." He shook his head. I believed him. I had to. Any other option left me fucked.

"What is it you think you're going to do?" Defiantly, Cyrus folded his arms over his chest. The rounded muscles in his shoulders and biceps flexed.

"Expel the cabrón. What do you think?" She went back to fidgeting with something.

"Ha, you think your trinkets and potions are going to do anything to Aeshma?"

"No, boy." She acted as though he'd said something ridiculous. "Truth." She pulled out what looked like a bronze plate.

"What the hell is that?" I questioned, strangely terrified of the disc she held in her hands.

"Sigil of Ameth," she said, her eyes wide, mesmerized by the thing.

"The Seal of God," Cyrus whispered.

"I knew this would one day come in handy. Your beast could only be overpowered by one thing. Truth. Obedience. Like that of God." Her face glowed by the shine of the metal disc. "Come. Sit on the floor." She motioned for me to come to her.

Mike and Cyrus moved in closer, but in true fashion, Dominika didn't budge in her indifference. If I made it out alive, her life would go on unaffected. Unless of course, I allowed her to join me in my destruction. Should Lupe lose and my beast consume me completely, she'd already staked her claim. Although I had a feeling the beasty didn't play well with others. Even other malicious beings.

"Do not enter the pentagram," Lupe commanded the boys. "Do not respond to her vile wickedness." She fiddled in her bag digging out more stuff. "Do you understand?" They each grumbled and nodded. "Let's begin."

She held the disc in front of her chest, eyes closed. Her lips moved speedily, but no words came out. I sat crisscross on the floor in the center of the star. Salt surrounded me but didn't seem to serve any obvious purpose.

"Lord God Almighty," she began. "Archangels in heaven. I call to you to bless the damned." She held the disc above my head. "Aeshma, I call to you." My hollow rumbled. "Ashmedai, I call to you." The thing inside me tumbled. "Show yourself," she demanded. The darkness inside moved about but didn't scurry to the surface. I was still, for all intents and purposes, me.

"Nothing's happening," I said, looking up at her. She turned away from me. "Maybe that thing is broken."

She turned back to face me. Her arm swung outward and splashed liquid across my face. I howled when the liquid seared my flesh.

"Ashmedai, I call to you," she repeated. "Show yourself."

My skin burned from the liquid. The hollow inside flamed to life and violently ripped its way out my throat. A bellowing howl tore through my throat, and my head flung back. "You call to me." My garbled voice replied to her. "You know not what you do." I heard my own voice intermingled with the gurgling rumbles of Ashmedai.

"Aeshma, in the name of the Lord God Almighty, I command you to exit this vessel." I laughed from deep within my belly. Veining tendrils of the beast wormed their way through my limbs. "Aeshma, the seal of God shines truth down upon you." I laughed again, this time lashing out at Lupe's legs with human claws. The moment my arm reached beyond the salt barrier, agonizing fire seared my skin. I jerked back in pain. Smoke rose from my burning flesh.

"God? What God?" I laughed while my flesh smoldered. "I am God."

"Water of Christ washes over you." She flung more acid into my face. I shrieked and fell back on the hardwood. Mike stepped forward, instincts kicking in to save me, but Cyrus's firm hand on his arm stopped him before he broke the circle.

"You think your water can stop me?" Deep and rumbling, my laugh sounded nothing close to human.

"Sraosha will stop you," Cyrus butted in from the sidelines.

My head twisted inhumanly fast to face him. Feral instinct began to roll over me. "That word does not frighten me."

"Sraosha breeds truth." He pushed on. Lupe continued to stand in front of me, but her eyes were focused on Cyrus who had promised to keep his trap shut. "May the demon of slothfulness which increases idleness, depart."

The hollow swelled, growing, pushing against the barriers

of each cell, until I thought it would burst from my skin. I howled, and the muscles in my back flexed, pulling me into an unnatural arch. Mike moved toward me again without thinking; this time Cyrus wasn't there to stop him. I flailed and screamed. Screamed until I tasted blood. Ashmedai writhed inside me at the sound of Cyrus's words. They seemed so simple, but the beast's agony ripped through my soul. Torso rising and falling from the floor, my heart thudded loudly, flip-flopping in my chest, only to be drowned out by my own shrieks. Lupe lowered the disc and stared at me. Cyrus had moved in close but didn't dare touch me. I could hear Mike breathing heavily to my left. The smell of his cologne wafted closer. Aeshma clambered for him, pleading for the healing powers brought by the devouring of our anchor.

I sat up straight and glared at him. Sweat dripped down my back. Uncontrollably, I lunged toward Mike, wailing. Without hesitation, he kicked the salt away and let me free. A moment before I reached him, he hit me with a right hook to the jaw. A cracking sound came just before the blackness.

My head bounced against Mike's back as he lumbered up the stairs. My fat ass flung over his shoulder, he heaved with each step. In his free hand, he held long strands of fabric. No one followed us. A few more steps, and we'd be alone in the bedroom at the top of the stairs.

Where I was headed I knew, why was anyone's guess. I'd been clocked on the side of the head and was being carried upstairs to the bedroom. My bedroom. My dead space.

Fake it.

The bedroom door swung open to the wall with a bang. I lay

still over his shoulder, not alerting him to my consciousness. The longer he thought I was out, the more time I had to formulate a plan. Very little of me was left inside, but what was there fought like hell to resurface. I'd done better on my own before fucked-up witch people called out my crazy.

Fake it.

We approached the bed. Only then did I pretend to wake up. "What? What happened?" I said softly.

He flipped me off his shoulder and onto the bed with a bounce. "I hit you. Sorry." Mike's indifference did nothing to my demonic passenger but what little pieces of me that were left behind ached.

I sat up on my elbows. Rubbing my face as though it hurt, I played up my injury. Since I'd healed my knife wound in the matter of an hour, a punch to the face proved to be nothing. "Why would you do a thing like that?" I asked, brows pulled upward in the center. We laid it on too thick, but Aeshma was desperate.

He looked away from me. His fear was gone and in its place was irreparable sadness. "Because no one else did anything."

"I-I don't even remember what happened before that," I lied.

"You went fucking bonkers." He worked the fabric in his hands. Fiddling with it as though he was waiting for the right moment to put them into use.

"Did it work?" The answer to that was a clear no.

Fake it.

He shrugged. "You tell me."

Sitting upright on the edge of the bed, I said, "I feel better." Forcing him to meet my eyes, I held his chin with a single hand on the side of his face. "Really. I do." *Lie.* "Can you just lay with me?" I pleaded kindly, reaching a hand out to hold his shoulder. "I'm just so tired."

He nodded softly. I scooted over, and Mike joined me on the bed. "I have no idea what's happening."

"Me either." I chuckled, and hell crept up my throat. I choked back the taste of sulfur.

"I don't know what to believe."

Definitely not me.

"Welcome to my world." His warm body lay close to mine. The smell of his cologne reminded Dylan Hart how badly she wanted to live a normal life and rid herself of the thing that squatted inside her. That thing, that beastly thing, Aeshma wanted nothing more than to revel in the slaughter of Detective Michael Petersen. Whatever bits of me still lingered inside were quickly being trampled by the beast as his thick veins consumed every inch of me. "Run," I pleaded. He didn't listen. "Run. Now." My panicked voice came a moment too late.

Hello, sweetie.

In a flash, I was on top of him. Thick legs straddled either side of his waist. "I've been waiting on you all day," I garbled.

His shocked eyes didn't know where to look as my hands rapidly lashed his wrists to the bedposts. I'd gotten mostly through his left hand when he figured out my ruse. Bucking wildly, he attempted to toss me off, but I was much too strong for him.

"Tsk, Tsk, Tsk," I clucked my tongue. "Don't try to fight me, boy," we garbled.

"Get the fuck out of her, you prick," he bawled, speaking only to my beast.

I cackled deep in my throat. "Keep wiggling, boy, this is thrilling." My body moved instinctively with his as he bucked.

Thick thighs clamped tight around his core. Rough denim rubbed raw my tender skin protected only by thin cotton panties. A guttural growl rolled up my chest. "Naughty boy." Leaning down closer to his face, I felt my expression change uncontrollably. His reaction told me whatever I was doing was scary as fuck. "Stop that now, or I'll have to remove this barrier between us." I reached a hand down between my legs to grope his crotch. "Settle down." The tip of my tongue flicked out and licked his lips. "This will only hurt for a second."

"Cyrus!" he screamed, lashing violently away from me. "Lupe! Help!"

My eyes rolled, and an exasperated sigh bubbled out. "Why did you have to go and do a thing like that? We were just starting to have fun."

"God," he cried out. He didn't believe in God. I knew that so the beast knew that. "Help me!" he begged. "Stop this." Tears formed at the edges of his eyes. "I love you," he said desperately. "Do you hear me? I love you. Babe, please."

I heard him loud and clear, but there wasn't a damn thing I could do about it. No matter how I tried to form words, they refused to come out. I screamed inside myself at the thing in control. A hot tear rolled down my face. Mike caught the glimmer, and his face changed.

"Stop, baby, please. Let me go. I can help you get better."

"You can help no one." My voice was my own again, but I wasn't in control of the words that came out.

"Yes, yes I can. You are bound to me, remember?" The desperation in his eyes tugged at my human, and I clawed at the nothingness that held me back. "Babe, I know you're in there somewhere. Fight." A sob shook his chest. "Fight or I'll die."

A fluttering from deep in my belly flittered up my core and bubbled out my mouth in the form of laughter. Maniacal, the chortling in my throat brought fear to Mike's eyes the glittered behind his tears. His strong arms strapped tight to the bedposts, he was weak and vulnerable, like a rosy-cheeked child ripe for the picking. The sickening idea that I wanted to take every last ounce of purity from the bottom of his soul both terrified me and tantalized the beast. What horrid things was I capable of? What atrocities could I commit if left unhindered?

I know.

"Kill me," I said quickly, forcing the beast away with all of my might. "Kill me now before you're all dead." Tears streamed down my face. Panic consumed me. I leaned down quickly and pressed my lips to his. My heart fluttered rapidly in my chest. Shuddering sobs pushed against my lips as I clung to him, to myself, to the earth.

My back arched violently while I straddled him, jerking me away from his kiss. Otherworldly screams echoed from my lungs. The stench of death belched from my throat. Aeshma ripped his way through my soul and finally overtook me completely. I couldn't hold him back any longer. My will was weak and my sins too great. I'd nourished him with my lies for days and he'd grown strong, stronger than my will, stronger than the power of Lupe and Cyrus. After all the running, after all the fighting, I was gone.

Fiery eyes fell on Mike, and he knew then and there I was gone. He screamed, loud and long. Called out for Lupe, for Cyrus, then finally for God. There was no God. Only me. I was too broken, too flawed, too weak to save him. To save myself. I hoped he'd kill me. Begged him silently to release my soul from the blackest depths of my psyche where Aeshma exiled me.

One strong, tight fist reared back and cracked loudly against his face. Mike's head shook with the force and immediately lolled to the side unconscious. His lips split, blood began to seep from the wound. I scurried down his legs to the foot of the bed, ignoring the copper scent that called to me, and secured his ankles to the posts. The world swam around me. I wanted to give in and let him have me, I didn't have the soul to fight him anymore. If I knew Mike would be safe, if I knew the world wouldn't come crashing down, I would have.

Cyrus and Lupe barreled into the room, clambering through the door side-by-side. Dominika sauntered in behind them. Cyrus held a small black take-out box in one hand and the seal of God in the other. Lupe gripped her bottle of acid, cigar still clenched between her teeth.

"We're too late," Cyrus said, his sorrowful tone lingered in the air like fog. "No." He shook his head as grief took him over. "No, this can't be."

My ragged breaths came heavy and panting. "What do you think you're going to do with that silly plate, boy?" I asked Cyrus about his bronze disc. Shaking his head, he couldn't form the words. "You think your trinkets and water can expel me?" I sniggered. "You are weak." I straddled Mike's legs near the foot of the bed. His body fully bound like a starfish to the oversized posts.

Save me. Please, someone, stop me.

Dominika sighed and snatched the box from Cyrus. "Since you've ruined them already," she said to him opening the box. "Have some fish, bitch." She began throwing small pieces of something fishy in my direction. The smell overpowered my hell stench, and Aeshma roared.

Bits of sushi fell to the floor around me as I lashed about

violently on top of Mike's legs. He never so much as opened an eye; out cold. Whatever plan Cyrus had made with the sushi, it was working. The beast inside scrambled around frantically to escape the barrage of fish and rice. In the moments Aeshma hid from the attack, I gained ground, forcing my own human soul into my limbs.

"Yes," Cyrus sneered at me while egging on Dominika's fishy assault. "I truly cannot believe this is working. The legends are true. This is all true." His voice held a disturbing air of astonishment and dismay. He darted toward me, leaning on one knee on the edge of the bed. "Smell that, asshole?" he probed the beast, drawing it out from where it hid away from the onslaught. "Fish." The smug smile I recalled seeing as he waved to me from the porch spread again across his face. "Would you like a taste?" He plucked a piece from the end of the bed and held it to my mouth. His poorly timed jab didn't amuse us, and we snarled spitefully at him, snapping our teeth in his face. Quickly, he smashed it against our lips. The beast cried out in pain and scurried away from the surface again. "We need more," he yelled frantically over his shoulder. "We must anoint her with them."

"No more, boss." Dominika shrugged from the doorway.

Fear washed over his face, and he turned back to meet my devilish eyes. "How can that be?"

"It was only leftovers, Cyrus. What do you want from me? Ask your magic woman to conjure up more."

"Dylan hold on, please." The desperation in his voice rolled over my skin and tugged at my soul. "Pick them up, quickly," he commanded Dominika.

I'm losing. I'm nearly lost.

The seal of God held tightly against his chest kept me and

my beast at bay for the moment. It had scampered away from the surface but still slithered through me like a slug, leaving behind a sticky trail that promised to keep my human soul trapped. Ashmedai wanted me, and he had me. Almost.

My tongue flicked rapidly against my control in Cyrus's direction. Rumbling and deep, a gurgling growl shook my chest. I lunged toward him, and he dropped the disk that had protected him. Cyrus leapt from the edge of the bed and skirted around the post. I slinked off Mike's legs and over the edge hands first, scuttling along the floor on all fours toward him. All the while growling and gnashing my teeth like a feral beast. Otherworldly noises rumbled in my chest. I was lost inside myself with no escape. I watched the people I cared about fearfully rush away from me, the hideous beast that pursued them.

Dominika didn't look back as she rushed out of the room, slamming the door behind her. Mike lay unconscious on the bed, bound to all four posts. Silent. Dead as far as I knew. The coppery scent of the blood that seeped slowly from his busted lip tickled my nose and fiery hunger brewed. Cyrus moved toward the door, hand clasped tightly around the knob. He'd leave Mike if it meant saving himself. He'd leave me if it came right down to it. Tied or not, Mike would have never left me. He would have died trying to save me from myself. He just might have.

Leaning on my knees, I lifted my chest, and a long guttural growl belched from my lungs. The stench of a thousand burning corpses filled the room. Cyrus coughed and covered his mouth and nose with his arm. Lupe did the same. Her wooden leg thudded against the floor as she swiftly made her way to the door to stop Cyrus.

"No, *mijo*. You cannot leave. We must stay strong." Lupe's rosary fell loosely around her hand. The shiny figure of Jesus on the wooded cross glinted in the dim light but did nothing to stop my advance.

"Your childish religion cannot stop me," I hissed, tongue flicking the air like a snake. The voice, a warbled demonic rendition of my own, I knew belonged to my shiny black demon. The one I'd sent packing before returning from hell. There was no denying the fact that my mission had failed. The fact was I would forever and always be cursed. Cursed to live in hell, trapped inside my own skin sack. Cursed to become the monster I was always destined to be.

Falling back to hands and knees, I scurried toward them, prepared to attack. Lupe held out the bronze plate, and I skidded to a stop. The door burst open behind Cyrus and Lupe. Cyrus stumbled toward me from the force of the door and stopped himself on his toes before falling. His beautiful green eyes locked onto mine. Wide and wild with a fear I'd never seen him possess. His arms spread wide, and he balanced himself to not fall to his knees in front of my gnashing teeth.

Ragged, sharp, panting breaths huffed in and out of my lungs. A sinister smile curled the corners of my mouth upward. I was predator and they were prey. Lupe and Cyrus were small game compared to the devilish being before me. Dominika sneered. Of all the souls in the room, we wanted hers.

"Your stench is vile, *Donnie*." We snarled at her. "Don't you growl at me, you rotten little beast." She scolded me as though I were a dog. Cyrus's face was still terrified, but Dominika seemed to, as usual, only care for herself. A sociopath if I'd ever seen one. Aeshma itched to claw his way up her legs and tickle her naughty bits while we ate her alive. My inner *Donnie* prayed she would be the one to stop the madness. I doubted Lupe would, Cyrus wouldn't, and Mike sure as fuck *couldn't.* I counted on the fact that if it really came down to it, Dominika would kill me. Death was the only solution to every problem.

Moving to balance on my hands and the balls of my feet, I leapt in her direction. The beast licked his chops, and I hoped she would put us down. I didn't want to die, but I sure as fuck didn't want to live in my possessed body forever. Dominika cocked a black brow in my direction. She'd tempted my demonic passenger and was left humiliated and unimpressed.

A phantom, whirling breeze kicked up anything not weighted down, Lupe's dress flittered with it exposing the tree stump she called a leg.

My muscles seared with the pain from forced, unnatural movement. I fought against Ashmedai with every ounce of my soul, but it pushed on unrelentingly. There was no discerning my actions from the will of the beast. We careened toward Dominika, me wanting to die, it wanting to take her with us. A scream, unnaturally brash and soulful, burst from my lungs and it was the beast, screeching at me to stop. We were about to die, or at the very least, we were about to rip Dominika a new asshole.

Hiking the hem of her skintight skirt, Dominika swung a long, lean leg in my direction. The pointed toe of her high heel made contact with my face. The bridge of my nose cracked, and blood promptly spewed across her pale white leg.

My head went first, then my torso. Laying over the backs of my own legs, my hips bent in an unnatural position. Half-conscious, blood dripping across my face, the sloppy wet gurgling of my demon laughed at them all. Back arching, my chest rose until my spine popped and cracked as I trembled with mirth.

Agony.

Have mercy on me.

I snarled as I laughed. "I will devour your forsaken soul, bitch."

Shallow, rapid breaths pushed my chest up, strangling me under the weight of my boobs as they nearly fell to my throat. The beat of a human heart that wasn't mine thudded in the distance. Without the beast, I would have never heard it. Wordlessly, I prayed that beating heart belonged to Mike.

Blood pooled under my eyes from my nose as I hung half over myself. Vision red, we closed our eyes against it. Hurried footsteps tromped the hardwood floor beside me. Death was on its way. Mine or theirs. The difference was a matter of moments and wherewithal.

Eyes closed, the scent of musky perfume mixed with my blood and smelled like a used pad. I gagged, and bile crept up my throat. Ashmedai enjoyed the scent and licked the air to taste it further.

"The beast that squats inside is devouring you from the inside out," Dominika suddenly whispered in my ear. Her heart was silent, if there was one at all. The beast roiled within. It lashed out to grasp what it desired. Dominika caught my arm and shoved it under her knees. "There's nothing left of you in there," she hissed. "Dylan Hart is gone. Killing you would be a favor, but your stowaway will need a new sinful host and it sure as fuck will not be me." Her voice was low and far away, I wondered if I was imagining her entirely.

Aeshma required another sinner to embody. The room was full of them. When I died, where would he go? Who would my beast choose?

"Dylan," Mike's husky, terrified voice abruptly called out to me amid the stench and thudding heartbeat. My soul trembled.

No.

My chin quivered. Mouth open to speak, pathetic whimpering shuddered up my throat. Jerking bed posts thudding against the hardwood floor. Grunts and the thumping of a terrified heart. I begged my body to cooperate. Pleaded with God for a last-second reprieve. No one would come to save me.

Life over. Promises broken.

Don't forget my human.

A sharp jab pierced my skin. Pressure engulfed the wound. Blood scented the air. Stillness of death surrounded me. Eyes remained closed, my body began to shut down. Mike's desperate whimpers, my final earthy sounds.

The world fell silent. Blackness took hold. Heart thumped sluggishly. Once, twice… too slow…

Exhale.

Stop.

I knew the bitch had it in her.

Several caught rats.

CPSIA information can be obtained
at www.ICGtesting.com
Printed in the USA
LVHW111629211022
731243LV00029B/1165/J

9 781735 863535